MUMMIES & MYSTERIES

A LIBRARY WITCH MYSTERY: BOOK 14

ELLE ADAMS

To be notified when Elle Adams's next book is released, sign up to her author newsletter.

1

On the day of Ivory Beach's much-anticipated Halloween party, I was unceremoniously jolted out of sleep by a large swathe of cobwebs landing on my head. I sat upright, struggling to disentangle myself, while Sylvester the owl cackled loudly from his perch on top of the doorframe.

With difficulty, I managed to tug the matted, sticky webs off my mouth so I could speak. "What did you do that for?"

"You were sleeping too peacefully," replied the owl. "I thought I'd fix it for you."

"Thanks." I pulled at the webbing, succeeding only in getting my hand and wrist just as tangled as my head. After several moments of struggling, I seized my wand from my bedside table and cast a removal spell. The webbing slid off my skin like soap, and I then shooed Sylvester out of my room so I could get dressed in peace.

Really, it was lucky that Xavier hadn't been here, or else he'd have been caught in the web as well—though the reasons for *that* were just as much of a cause for annoyance as my unwelcome early awakening. Admittedly, Xavier could slip out of Sylvester's fake webs without needing to use magic at all. One of many perks of being a Reaper.

When I'd showered and dressed, I went downstairs to the kitchen. Estelle sat eating cornflakes at the table, while Sylvester perched beside her bowl and blinked his big owl eyes innocently at me. Someone—Aunt Adelaide, no doubt—had left a stack of toast on a plate next to jars of jam and marmalade and a full coffeepot.

"Hey, Estelle." I picked up a plate of my own and piled toast onto it. "Ready for tonight?"

"I *hope* so." She rubbed her tired eyes. "My mum's double-checking I didn't leave anything off the list, but my main concern is that we won't have enough time between the library closing and the event's grand opening. Oh, and making sure nobody unexpected shows up without being invited."

She meant the vampires. Which was a risk, I'd admit, but Estelle had been planning the library's annual Halloween party since *last* year, and we didn't need to let a group of fanged nuisances ruin the night.

Sylvester stole a piece of toast from my plate. "If you don't want unexpected people to show up, don't host a masquerade ball open to the public."

Without waiting for a reply, he took flight in a feathery swoop, dropping a trail of crumbs onto my head as he did so.

I shook my head to dislodge them and gave Estelle an encouraging smile. "Ignore him. He's in a mood today. He woke me up by throwing cobwebs onto my face."

Estelle sighed. "I know he's right, though. I just thought… I mean, we've spent long enough lying low. It's not like we don't have any defences against potential trouble in here."

"Exactly." I began buttering my toast. "Maybe Sylvester has a touch of stage fright and is taking it out on the rest of us."

Estelle snorted. "That'll be the day."

For reasons known only to his enigmatic self, Sylvester had bargained—or manipulated—his way into becoming the starring attraction of the night. Given his usual habit of staying hidden from the public eye, for the most part, I wasn't sure why he'd suddenly become attached to the idea of performing at the library's biggest annual event. Since the owl had an undeniable flair for the dramatic, though, I was sure that he'd get over his nerves and wow everyone tonight.

"Could be worse," I added. "At least we didn't go with a vampire-specific theme like Aunt Candace suggested."

"That'd have got Evangeline's hackles up," Estelle agreed. "Got to make sure we stay on good terms with our fanged neighbours. Do you think she'll show up tonight?"

"Highly unlikely." We were too low-class for the local vampires, despite a masquerade ball being exactly their cup of tea—or wineglass of blood. Either worked.

It wasn't the local vampires who concerned me, though. Evangeline and I would never be close friends, but she didn't belong to the group of rogues with an unending grudge against my family and who might take tonight's event as an invitation to make trouble. We'd driven them out of the library several times already, but it'd be nice to have a stress-free night—or as stress-free as possible for a family of biblio-witches anyway.

Estelle brushed crumbs off her lap. "It's too late now, and Sylvester knows it too. We've already put out the word, and half the town's promised to attend. Maybe more. Depends how many other parties there are tonight."

"I can't imagine most of them will be invited to Evangeline's." Her events were the very definition of exclusive—and not generally human friendly either. "No, we'll be fine. Between the library's defences and the threat of being pecked to death by an owl, nobody will dare make trouble tonight."

Estelle and I finished breakfast and left our family's living quarters for the main part of the library, where the lobby was decked out, ready for the evening. The centrepiece, a giant inflatable pumpkin, hovered above, level with the ceiling. Below, three storeys of shelves climbed upwards, draped in spiderwebs and fringed with orange-and-black tinsel.

Sylvester perched on the topmost balcony, directly below the pumpkin, which he surveyed with a greedy eye. After he'd spent weeks popping any balloon Estelle left unattended, she'd finally wrangled him into an agreement where he was allowed to burst the giant pumpkin balloon at the beginning of the party on the condition that he left it alone beforehand. Neither Estelle nor I had entirely had faith in him to exercise restraint, and I knew she had at least two other pumpkins waiting in the wings as backup.

When he saw me looking at him, Sylvester shuffled his feet around but left his face turned towards us in that creepy owl-like manner. He did not, however, make a move for the pumpkin.

"He's behaving," said Aunt Adelaide, emerging from behind a shelf with her arms full of fake cobwebs. Tall and curvy, she resembled her daughter, Estelle, and shared her head for business too. "He's been sitting up there for most of the night and hasn't touched anything."

"Good." Spying a pile of books waiting in the box next to the front desk, I went to organise them.

"Oh, you don't have to bother with the returns, Rory," added my aunt, siphoning off the cobwebs with an expert wave of her wand. Somehow, she'd avoided getting any tangled in her long, curly red hair. "I'll handle them."

"It's no big deal," I insisted. "You and Estelle already have enough to do."

The pair of them had put this event together in a matter of weeks, an impressive achievement with the number of setbacks that had stood in their way. Between vampiric threats and vanishing corridors, magical libraries came with all sorts of hazards at the best of times. I'd been living here for less than a year, so there were some areas that I didn't have access to yet, and the gaping holes in my magical knowledge became apparent when faced with a new challenge, like a Halloween party, for instance.

I placed the pile of returns on the desk and reached for the roll of parchment that listed all the codes and their corresponding sections. I'd got pretty good at finding the main ones without needing to consult a guide, but there was usually one oddity in there.

"Hey, Jet," I called my familiar's name. "Can you help me with these?"

"Here, partner!" he squeaked, fluttering down to my shoulder. The little crow wasn't strong enough to lift a book larger than a pamphlet, but he liked to participate in the library's activities, and I figured I might as well tire him out a little before the party. Yesterday, he'd got himself worked up into such a frenzy over the upcoming celebrations that I'd had to ban him from flying around the Reading Corner and distracting the visitors by twittering at them. My family alone could understand his speech, a trait he shared with Sylvester. Aside from that and the wings, the pair had absolutely nothing else in common.

"This way." I picked up the first return—a large magical dictionary—and carried it through the reference section, which stretched behind the front desk. Generally, the shelves down here stayed where they were put, though I did have to move one of Aunt Candace's notebooks from the dictionaries section where she'd stashed it on a shelf.

Typically, when I picked up the notebook, my hand turned bright purple. *Security spell, is it?* Since it was my wand hand that had been affected, I reached for my Biblio-Witch

Inventory instead. The little book I kept in my pocket came in handy in situations involving simple spells, where I could usually just press my fingertip to the pre-written word *reverse* and undo whatever prank had hit me.

Notably, Aunt Candace herself was nowhere to be seen. She'd likely either be plotting a Halloween-themed novel to add to her collection or else assembling her outfit for the evening. That left Cass, who was up on the third floor with an array of magical monsters. I fervently hoped her pets would *not* be participating in the event, though a kelpie rampaging around would certainly add to the Halloween atmosphere.

When I walked out of the research division to pick up the next book, I spied Estelle fixing a banner across the first-floor balcony while Spark the pixie helped hang up the other end. The little fairy was scarcely bigger than my palm, his wings as delicate as the fake cobwebs, but he held the banner valiantly in his tiny fingers.

"Need a hand?" I called up to them.

"I'm all right." Estelle adjusted the banner and stepped back. "The banners keep falling down. I blame Sylvester for sharpening his claws on them."

"Why not stick them on with cobwebs?" I suggested. "I'd like to see him disentangle his claws from that."

"He'd put mice in my bed for a week if I did that to him." She beckoned Spark back to her side, and the little pixie perched on her shoulder. "Though I guess if I warn him in advance, he'll only have himself to blame."

"Exactly." I was impressed at how quickly she'd managed to drape the library in decorations, given Sylvester's apparent attempts to undo her progress. "Anything else you need help with?"

"Yes—we'll have to seal off the third floor tonight," she said. "We can't have anyone getting into the fourth-floor corridor. I don't think Cass will want them getting near her animals either."

"Definitely not," I said firmly. "She won't decide to shake things up by letting one of her magical monsters loose, will she?"

"Not after Mum chewed her out the last time," said Estelle.

"She didn't, did she?" Sensing a story there, I asked, "Not the kelpie?"

"No, but ten years ago, Cass brought a baby pegasus to the Halloween party. It ate three books."

"Ouch." Cass had been on her best behaviour lately, though her patience might be put under strain when faced with the choice between being shut out of the Magical Creatures Division during the event or being locked in with the monsters. Knowing her, though, I was sure she'd choose the latter. There was no way we could risk any of the guests getting into the entrance to the fourth-floor corridor. While the guardian stood in place to keep out intruders, we didn't need the library's resident shadowy monster to crash the party any more than we needed a manticore on the loose.

I picked up three books from the returns section that needed to be taken to the third floor and then made for the stairs. No books were registered as belonging on the fourth floor, and the corridor had inexplicably vanished several decades ago thanks to my late grandmother's highly effective concealment and misdirection spells. The corridor's recent rediscovery had also awakened its guardian, a being that had been created to guard the corridor against anyone who didn't belong to our family and the reason we'd have to take pains to ensure nobody from the party wandered upstairs by mistake.

The guardian's magic paled in comparison to that which it guarded. The fourth floor concealed a room that could grant the wish of any of us who asked for their heart's desire, within certain parameters. That the room worked for my family alone didn't mean we wanted the whole world to know, especially certain vampires who coveted rare magic like magpies collected shiny objects.

Speaking of rare magic...

"Estelle!" I called out. "What about the Book of Questions?"

"What about it?" she called back.

"We're not leaving it in its usual place, are we?"

"Of course not," she replied. "My mum's sealing it in a downstairs room where nobody can get their hands on it."

"Good." I'd wanted to check, as the Book of Questions was amongst the most dangerous of the library's artefacts—and that was among some serious competition. Like the corridor, its magic was restricted to my family members alone, but I shuddered to think what Sylvester might do to any unwitting guest who opened its pages. *Turn them into a footstool, probably.*

When I reached the third floor, I went in search of Cass. A warning growl from behind the door to the Magical Creatures Division told me the manticore's cage was open, so I knocked first in case I found myself trapped between the jaws of a half-lion, half-crocodile.

"What?" she called. "Rory, is it? Come in and stop lurking."

"Just wanted to make sure your pet wasn't loose." I nudged open the door and stepped inside, keeping a safe distance from the cage at the back, near which Cass stood. Her sleeves were rolled to the elbows and her red hair twisted into a messy knot behind her head, while the manticore's crocodilian tail was visible in the cage behind her.

"The others wanted to ask if you were okay with our

blocking off the stairs to the third floor tonight," I said. "To make sure none of the guests can get up here."

She barely blinked. "And you thought you needed to ask me… why?"

Surely she'd guessed. "Are you going to stay up here while the party is going on?"

"Yes, I'll stay," she said crisply. "I don't think I'll be missing much if I skip out on the party. I have all the entertainment I need."

"Fair enough." At an ominous growl from the manticore, I stepped out the door. "I thought I'd be polite and ask before we locked you upstairs. You really don't mind?"

"Of course not."

Only Cass would prefer being in a monster's cage to a party. In fairness, I'd usually rather be reading a book instead, but tonight was as much a celebration for me as everyone else. Part of me had thought Cass might feel the same, but I'd once again underestimated her devotion to all things scaled and clawed.

I finished returning the books and got on with the work of the day. Between helping with preparations and listening to my familiar spread gossip from the rest of town about who was coming to the event tonight, the hours raced by, and before we knew it, our closing time was upon us. As evening approached, we did a last sweep of the library to turf out any stragglers reading in the corners before we closed the doors and went to our respective rooms to get ready.

For my costume, I'd picked out a black dress Cass had loaned me and then bought a mask that resembled a crow's feathers so I'd match my familiar—simple enough. My phone pinged with a rare message as I fit the mask into place, and a familiar ache hit my chest to see Xavier's name. He was the one person I could all but count on to *not* show up tonight, thanks to his boss the Grim Reaper's inherent disapproval of our relationship and the fact that Halloween was known for being a busy one for Reapers. His message—*have fun tonight*—brought a familiar bittersweet tang, but I tried to take it to heart. Xavier didn't want me to spend the night moping instead of celebrating with my family.

When I left my room, Laney slipped out into the corridor with a vampire's swift grace, her dark-brown hair bouncing to her shoulders. Relieved tears pricked my eyes, the same reaction I'd had every time I'd seen her for the past week, since she'd woken from a coma that I'd feared was permanent. That had been my first wish granted by the fourth-floor corridor: to wake her up from the effects of the poison she'd mistakenly ingested trying to save my life from one of the Founders, and her recovery was the reason tonight was as much a celebration for my family as it was a fun night for the rest of town.

That was, if the Founders didn't show up tonight to finish the job.

I slammed a lid on those thoughts and fixed on a smile. "Hey, Laney. You're coming to the party?"

"I wouldn't miss it." The slightest hint of fang poked out from her mouth when she smiled, but she came by those naturally, with no need to wear a costume.

"Aren't you dressing up?" I asked.

"I don't have anything to wear," she said. "Unless someone has a spare outfit?"

"I'm sure Cass would lend you one."

Laney pulled a face. "No, thanks."

"Then I'll ask Estelle." It didn't matter too much if Laney didn't dress up—frankly, everyone else being in masks would be enough of a recipe for confusion already—but Cass wouldn't mind her borrowing something. *I think.* Cass's attitude towards Laney had been perplexing, to say the least, since Laney had awoken from her coma.

Downstairs, I found Estelle cleaning up the remains of a dead mouse from the front desk. "Ugh. Was that Sylvester?"

"I think he was trying to add to the atmosphere." She made the mouse vanish with a wave of her wand. "Oh, hey, Laney. Not dressing up?"

"She doesn't have a costume," I explained. "I was going to ask if you had a spare."

"Oh, I can resize one of my old outfits. No problem," Estelle said. "Come with me, Laney."

"I'll make sure Sylvester doesn't behead any more rodents," I offered. "We don't need that trauma."

The owl didn't technically need to eat due to not being alive in any literal sense, but my "stage fright" theory might have merit with how erratically he was behaving today. I wouldn't lie—I was pretty nervous, too, while Jet had got himself so overexcited that I found him flying in circles at warp speed until he nearly knocked himself out on a book-shelf. Aunt Adelaide rescued him by gently extending a hand and scooping him up.

"Careful," she said. "Rory, you look wonderful."

"Thanks." I smiled. "Aren't you going to get ready? I can keep an eye on things down here."

"I'll do it, partner!" Jet squeaked, bouncing up and down on her hand like a yo-yo.

"Okay, but don't hurt yourself." I ran through the mental list of people who should be present. "Should someone check on Aunt Candace?"

"Can you do that, Rory?" Aunt Adelaide asked with an apology in her voice. "If she's got lost in her manuscript, she'll appreciate a reminder that she'll need to get ready."

"Sure." I headed back to the living quarters and made for the staircase leading up to our rooms. The room at the top was Aunt Candace's writing cave, and I never knew quite what I'd open the door on, so I knocked first. "Aunt Candace, are you ready?"

Her voice drifted upward from the floor below. "No, I can't find my outfit!"

I followed her voice down to the door that led to her actual bedroom, in which she spent surprisingly little time. I entered to find a scene that looked like there'd been an explosion in a fancy-dress shop. A pirate outfit lay next to the upper half of a tiger costume, while various wigs were heaped in a hairy pile in the middle of the floor. A tutu hung from the ceiling, adorned with feathers like a tropical bird.

Aunt Candace was dressed from head to toe in a greyish outfit that resembled a mummy, but she had no mask on, and her wildly curly red hair hung down to her shoulders. "My mask has gone missing!"

"Which mask?" Pretty much any mask would go with her current outfit, which was surprisingly drab compared to her normal style. She usually wore bright flowery skirts and dresses, but she'd opted for clothing that was more suited to a prison cell than a party.

She clucked her teeth. "I bet my sister stole it."

"Stole what?" Aunt Adelaide asked from the doorway. "What've you got yourself worked up over?"

"She says she can't find her outfit," I replied. "No idea what she's talking about."

"My sister knows," said Aunt Candace. "She's had it in for my special mask from the start."

"Not *that* mask." Aunt Adelaide gave a quiet groan. "Couldn't you pick one that isn't—?"

"It isn't cursed," Aunt Candace interrupted. "Really, you people have no sense of adventure."

"Cursed or not, it's hideous."

"Cursed?" I raised a brow at Aunt Candace. "You have a cursed mask?"

"I *had* a not-cursed mask," she corrected me. "Which someone stole."

"It probably moved by itself," said Aunt Adelaide. "I haven't touched it, Candace. I have better things to do with my time."

"If she'd touched it, she'd probably have purple hands," I told Aunt Candace, recalling the notebook incident earlier. "Thanks for that, by the way."

"You're welcome."

I rolled my eyes then left my aunt to resume the search and returned to the lobby. Estelle and Laney joined me a minute later, the former dressed in an adorable fairy outfit that closely matched Spark the pixie, the latter in a slinky dress and an ornate feathered mask that covered her eyes but not her fangs.

After a short while, Aunt Adelaide came downstairs dressed in an even more elegant version of Laney's feathery ensemble, bedecked in jewels and vibrant feathers.

"Sylvester," she called up to the balcony. "Ready? It's almost time."

"I've been ready for hours, you cauliflower," came the reply.

As the seconds ticked down to nine o'clock, Aunt Candace finally came bounding in from the living quarters, announcing, "I found the mask under the bed. I knew it'd be somewhere."

The mask in question looked like it was made of dead skin. Certainly not my first choice for a costume party, though it was thematically appropriate, and it distracted attention from the notebook and pen bobbing up and down at her side. No doubt she'd be mining the guests for ideas all night.

"Everyone ready?" Estelle asked for the fifth time.

"Yep," I said, and Aunt Adelaide and Laney echoed my sentiment.

A rush of pride and happiness bolstered me. My family was reunited, and together, we'd be able to face anything that might happen tonight.

2

As the clocks struck nine, the library's doors swung open to let in the first guests. In an instant, a crowd of masked and enthusiastic visitors sailed into the library. First to enter were a group of students from the university dressed up as werewolves, who went straight to the snack table next to the large open space we'd designated as the dance floor.

Behind them came a group of witches dressed as various woodland animals. I saw Zee from the bakery, who was recognisable by her curly hair poking out from behind a cat-eared mask, but other than that, I didn't have a clue who any of these people were. From my position at the foot of the stairs, I edged closer to Laney.

"See anyone we know?" I asked in a whisper.

"You know more of the locals than I do."

"Yes, but everyone's in costume."

Laney had sharper senses than I did, but they were hard to employ in such a large crowd, and the masks added a new level of confusion. My own mask was fairly practical, but I had to dodge a gangly wizard who'd worn a mask covered in so many fake eyeballs that he kept tripping headlong over his own feet.

I gave a double take when someone walked past wearing a flat black mask and cloak and carrying a scythe, but they weren't the right height for the real Grim Reaper.

Laney followed my gaze. "Xavier isn't coming?"

"No, the Grim Reaper is still being grouchy." My heart gave a pang, though I'd resolved not to let Xavier's absence ruin the night.

"Typical," she said. "That guy doesn't need a costume to be part of this show. All he'd have to do is lurk in the background."

"Yeah, but I'm told the Reapers have a busy time on Halloween, what with amateurs trying to summon the dead." It was more than that, of course. I'd broken the implicit agreement between the three of us when I'd called Xavier to my rescue in a tight spot when dealing with the Founders, and the Grim Reaper was not known for forgiveness. But I didn't want to bring down the mood by reminding Laney that the reason I'd got that close to the Founders in the first place was because I'd been desperately trying to save her from the poison that had put her in a coma.

"He'd probably take someone dressing up as him as a grave insult," said Laney. "Pun intended."

My heart gave a jolt when I spied the first vampire costume. I'd kind of hoped the townspeople would be reticent to annoy Evangeline, but I guessed they'd assumed she and her fellow vampires wouldn't come to the party—which was a fair assumption, since she'd made it clear that we'd never match up to her standards.

Seeing my reaction, Laney nudged me. "Relax. She's a werewolf, not a vampire. I'd know if there were any real vampires here."

"Right, of course." I felt myself flush. "I wish they'd gone with a regular fancy dress theme, without the masks, though. I'm still a little jumpy."

My mind unwittingly conjured up an image of one of the Founders' parties, where vampires mingled with normals who had no idea their hosts deeply desired to sink their fangs into their unwary guests. I took in several calming breaths, reminding myself that I'd always recognise my family members even while masked and that they had their eyes wide open for trouble. Estelle and Aunt Adelaide stood on either side of the dance floor, waving at the guests as they walked in, while Aunt Candace lurked in a corner, her notebook and pen bouncing up and down at her side and her hideous mask looking even more ominous in the low lighting.

Personally, I thought the library's decor easily rivalled the vampires' home at its best. Pumpkin-shaped lanterns hovered level with the shelves above the open space of the lobby, and the cobwebs draped over the balconies glowed in the dark too.

"Looks like half the town is here," Laney murmured. "Wasn't anyone else throwing a party tonight?"

"Not on this scale." Estelle had really outdone herself, and while I was happy for her, it came as a relief when the tide of visitors slowed enough for the doors to close, and a bright spotlight shone upon the corner where my cousin stood waiting to greet everyone.

"Welcome to the party!" Estelle said into a microphone. "It's great to see you all here. I know this is an important night for the witch covens, but I thought we deserved our own little celebration too."

Several cheers ensued, and as the audience broke into applause, I saw Estelle blush underneath her feathered mask.

"I have a special announcement to make," she went on then paused for dramatic effect. "The festivities will be kicked off by none other than our family's familiar, Sylvester."

All eyes went to the ceiling as the spotlight moved to point directly upward at the giant inflatable pumpkin. Sylvester took flight from the balcony, his wings spread outward to cast a long shadow over the dance floor. When his beak pierced the giant pumpkin, a deafening bang rang through the library. Everyone shrieked and covered their ears or jumped, and as the pumpkin burst, a torrent of glittering confetti rained down on their heads.

"Look carefully!" Estelle raised her voice into the microphone. "There are a few pieces of paper hidden amongst the confetti, and one of them contains a special message."

The guests lowered their hands to catch the confetti, while Sylvester flew in circles above, through the wreckage of the inflatable pumpkin.

"If you find the paper that has the word *congratulations* written on it, come and see me, and I'll give you a prize," Estelle told the crowd. "Have a great night, everyone!"

Enthusiastic cheers answered, and while the spotlight died down, there came a lot of scrambling to pick up the papers in the hopes of uncovering the prize.

"What if the paper landed in someone's drink or something?" Laney whispered to me. "Or in the punch bowl?"

"Someone'll fish it out." Nobody could resist the promise of a mystery prize, in my experience.

Sure enough, after a few minutes of excited scrambling, someone shouted in triumph.

"I won!" A wizard—or I thought he was a wizard, though he was dressed as a mummy and draped in bandages—ran towards Estelle, waving a paper in the air. "I won!"

"Oh, come on. That's not fair," a nearby woman said in a carrying whisper. "Hasn't he already had enough wins in the past week? He should give it to someone else."

Estelle waved her wand and conjured up a giant cuddly toy pumpkin, which she presented to the winner. Some people cheered or groaned in disappointment, but the sound was soon lost in the clamour as music blasted out of the speakers. Without further ado, the lights went down, and the party began in earnest.

If anyone else had complaints, I didn't hear them amidst the cheerful, dancing crowd. Generally, I preferred staying indoors with a good book to partying. I'd spent most of the past few weeks wracked with guilt over Laney, and to see her throwing herself into the mood with abandon was worth the inevitable introvert hangover I'd have for the rest of the week. Estelle had pulled out all the stops, and the library was perfect for this kind of event.

Laney even managed to drag me up to dance for a while, too, though I soon got tired of tripping over my feet and went to sit down. I found myself next to the snack table with Aunt Candace, who was similarly avoiding the dance floor. Her notebook and pen were hard at work, taking notes on people's costumes, and I was willing to bet she'd already concocted some new ideas for stories.

"There you are," said Aunt Candace. "Your Reaper friend isn't here?"

"You know the Grim Reaper doesn't approve of parties." My mood dimmed a little, though I tried to keep my tone light. "Can you imagine him dancing in a conga line?"

"I expect he's busy," Aunt Candace said with a laugh. "Reapers have their work cut out for them on Halloween. Someone always tries to contact the dead and ends up with an unwanted spirit inside their house."

"Just as long as they don't do it in the library." You'd think people would think twice about risking being on the wrong side of the Grim Reaper's scythe.

"You never know," she said. "A ghost might bring a bit of excitement."

"Isn't this exciting enough for you?"

"On Samhain, the boundaries between life and death are thinner than usual." She dropped her voice to an eerie whisper. "Sometimes, entities come back from the other side to haunt the living."

"Not in the library, I hope." That was an unsettling thought. Her creepy mask didn't help matters, either, and I was starting to wish I'd picked a different corner to sit in. "Sylvester wouldn't stand for it."

She gave a prolonged sigh. "I suppose not."

I glanced at her mask, suppressing a shudder at the creepy dead skin. "That's not real skin, is it?"

"It wouldn't be much of a costume if it wasn't."

Sensing the need to extricate myself from the conversation, I returned to the dance floor and accidentally ended up in a conga line with a group of people dressed as zombies who had entirely too little concept of personal space. To my great relief, Estelle rescued me, reaching out a hand to pull my flailing body out of the line.

"They're a little *too* realistic," she remarked, waving her wand to remove fake blood from her hair. "Everyone's gone all out on the costumes. I'm surprised."

"I'm not. People like an excuse to dress up." That and the weather had been so dismal recently that nobody wanted to spend time outdoors, so an indoor party was ideal for this time of year.

"I guess they do." She grinned under her mask. "Laney's having a good time."

"I'm glad." Seeing her happiness brought my mood right back up. "Someone needs to drag Aunt Candace onto the dance floor too."

"What's she doing?"

"Sitting in the corner in her creepy mask, morbidly wishing some ghosts would show up."

"There's that guy, but I don't think he's making much of an effort with his costume." Estelle pointed at someone who kept tripping over the edges of his white-sheet costume.

"No kidding." I was about to ask where Aunt Adelaide was when I spotted her leading the conga line, her glittery mask shining below the floating lights near the ceiling.

Movement on the balcony made me raise my head, and I made out the shadowy form of Cass peering down from the third floor. I hoped she hadn't had second thoughts about being shut upstairs, but knowing her, I was sure she was happier with her monsters inside their cage.

When the conga line finally ran out of steam, Estelle retrieved the microphone and bounded to address the crowd again. "Hey, everyone. I hope you're having fun!"

An array of enthusiastic cheers responded.

"Good," she said when the cheers had faded out. "We're going to have our karaoke contest now. The best singer will win another prize!"

Aunt Candace groaned so audibly that I jumped, not realising she'd been lurking behind me. "I *hate* karaoke."

"Really?" I'd have thought karaoke would be right up her street, albeit as a spectator, not a participant. "Why?"

"Because it's tiresome to listen to people who can't sing," she said. "At least if they *can* sing, you can safely ignore them."

I rolled my eyes. "Are you going back to your room, then?"

"Oh, no, I won't miss it."

Honestly. I went in search of Laney instead, and we watched a series of wizards, witches, werewolves, and others step up to the microphone. Most were drunk or at least slightly tipsy, which made for some interesting performances. Even Aunt Adelaide sang a surprisingly heartfelt edition of "My Heart Will Go On," while Laney sauntered up to the stage and sang "Girls Just Want to Have Fun" so well that everyone broke out in spontaneous applause.

When Estelle called on everyone to vote on the winner, they unanimously picked Laney. While I was sure some vampire effects were involved in how she'd sung, nobody seemed bothered, and they cheered again when Laney stepped up to take her prize from Estelle. Grinning, she waved the cuddly bat she'd won to the crowd and then went back to dancing when the music started up again.

My legs had begun to ache by then, so I found an empty seat, but I hastily vacated it when a feather fell on my head. When I glimpsed Sylvester perched on the balcony above, I moved further away in case he dropped a dead mouse next. I hoped he'd got enough fun out of popping the balloon and that he wouldn't try any pranks, but everyone was in such a buoyant mood that it might not necessarily matter.

Since a few guests had begun to depart, I stood near the door to make sure nobody tripped down the stairs on the way out. Midnight approached, and the only person who appeared to come more alive with each passing hour was Laney—which was reassuring in a way, since it all but proved she was the only vampire present. As for me, I had to keep pacing to keep from dozing off. My introvert battery was officially depleted, and my face ached from smiling.

Since I was standing right next to the front, I was amongst the first to hear the clamour and shouts from outside. I startled into full wakefulness when the door flew wide open, inviting in a blast of cold night air and a cry of "Murder!"

"What?" I ran into the doorway. "Did you say… murder?"

"Someone's dead!" A breathless man climbed the stairs, his face hidden behind a mask covered in fake eyeballs.

"Who?" I glanced behind me, my mouth going dry.

The guests continued to dance, most of them overlooking the interruption.

"Are you sure they aren't just drunk?" Laney came gliding up to join me, her vampire hearing having easily picked up on our conversation. "Who is it?"

"I don't know!" The man wrung his hands, the fake eyeballs bouncing up and down on his mask. "I nearly tripped over him lying in the street when I was on my way home."

Aunt Adelaide appeared on the doorstep too. "Is something wrong?"

"There's a body!" repeated the eyeball-masked guy. "I think it's one of your guests."

"Oh no." Aunt Adelaide removed her mask, revealing smudged makeup around her eyes. "Where?"

"There." He pointed across the square and down the road that led to the seafront. I couldn't see anything from here, but the library's dim lights barely reached the front steps, and the town square was swathed in darkness.

"Did you call the police?" I asked. "Someone needs to fetch Edwin."

Not just him. If someone had really died, either the Grim Reaper or Xavier would be coming to collect their soul. For everyone's sakes—and for selfish reasons, too, I'd admit—I hoped it'd be the latter.

"What's going on?" Estelle ran over to join us, her makeup running down her sweaty face underneath her mask. "Why's everyone out here?"

"He found a body, apparently," Aunt Adelaide told her in an undertone. "One of the partygoers."

"This way." The eyeball-masked man beckoned to us. "I know I should have gone to the police first, but I wasn't sure anyone was in the office tonight."

"Edwin should be there," said Estelle. "I'll come with you."

"No, I will," I said quickly. "You should stay at the party."

"If one of my guests is hurt, I need to check he's okay." Estelle stepped forward. "Mum, can you watch the party?"

"Of course." Aunt Adelaide retreated into the library.

"You should go too," I whispered to Laney. "Best not to wander around town after dark."

"What? You think Evangeline'll get jealous that I picked your party over hers?"

"She's having a party?" My heart gave an uneasy swoop at the memory of the last event I'd attended at the vampires' home.

"No, she's gone to someone else's," said Laney in a whisper. "Out of town. I turned down her invitation."

"Good." I gave myself a mental shake. A body didn't mean a vampire attack. Evangeline's people were better behaved than that, and they took great care to make sure that no rogue vampires trespassed in town.

"It'll be fine." Laney gave me a reassuring smile. "I'll wait for you here and make sure the other guests behave themselves."

"Thanks." Estelle would need the moral support. "I'll be back soon."

I fell into step with Estelle, who'd pulled off her mask. Her expression was crestfallen as she followed the eyeball-masked guy across the darkened square.

"The man might be fine," I whispered to her. "I don't see the Reaper. Either of them."

"That doesn't mean they haven't been here," she murmured back. "Unless you've heard from Xavier…?"

I shook my head. "Not since before the party."

If he and the Grim Reaper were out of town, a dead body would summon them back, but while I'd wanted to see Xavier tonight, murder had been the last thing on my mind.

3

Estelle and I followed the eyeball-masked guy, who turned out to be called Terrance Lindon. While we'd tried not to draw too much attention from inside the library, a handful of other guests had wandered out to see what was going on or doubled back from walking home out of curiosity.

By the time we reached the side street next to the clock tower, we'd drawn a dozen masked and costumed onlookers. Halting, Terrance pointed at a body dressed in plain black, which lay surrounded by what appeared to be bandages. It took me a moment to figure out the guy had been dressed as a mummy, though his mask had slipped downward, and the only bandages still on his body were wrapped around his neck.

"Did someone strangle him with his own costume?" I whispered to Estelle.

"I… I think so." She glanced uneasily at the gathering guests. "We need to fetch the…"

I assumed she'd been going to say "police," but her sentence trailed off when a large shadow fell over the street.

A hooded figure swooped upon the body, and the onlookers retreated with gasps and shouts.

Only I remained, even as the hooded figure bent over the body and a transparent outline resembling the dead man on the ground drifted upward without seeming to notice he had an audience. When the hooded figure beckoned with a crooked hand, a large door-like gap appeared in the swathe of darkness, opening with a chill wind that reached me even at the mouth of the alley. I shivered, teeth chattering, while the transparent form of the dead man drifted towards the emptiness. The instant the ghost vanished through the door, both melted away into the surrounding darkness. Then the hooded figure turned to me, holding a long, curved scythe.

If I didn't know him as my boyfriend, I'd have taken a step back at the sheer menacing nature of his Reaper appearance. As it was…

"Rory." The shadows faded, properly revealing Xavier's blond hair and aquamarine eyes. "What are you doing here?"

"That man… he was one of our guests. At the party." There was a lot more I wanted to say but not out in public next to a body and a bunch of onlookers who'd watched him Reap a dead man's soul. "Did he say anything to you? I mean, did he see whoever killed him?"

"No, I assumed he was ambushed from behind," said Xavier. "I should have asked, but I didn't think…"

"I'd be here?" Regret swelled in my throat. I wished we were alone, if just because I was curious to know what had taken him longer than usual to show up to claim the guy's soul. He and his boss must have been out of town—but where?

Xavier opened his mouth to reply and then closed it when someone shined a torch into the street, illuminating the body on the ground. Sudden recognition dawned on me when I properly saw his face.

"Estelle?" I spied her approaching, tailed by several guests whose curiosity had evidently overtaken the shock of the Reaper's appearance. "Estelle—isn't he the guy who won that prize from Sylvester's raffle?"

"Oh." Estelle pressed a hand to her mouth. "Yes... but where is it?"

"What prize?" asked Xavier.

"There was a contest..." I looked around the street, but I didn't see any signs of the cuddly pumpkin the victim had won. Had someone stolen it? It struck me as kind of harsh to steal from a dead man, though for all I knew, the same person had been responsible for his death.

Admittedly, it was highly unlikely that he'd been murdered for the sake of a toy pumpkin. *Right?*

"A contest at the party," Estelle added then turned towards the gathering crowd. "Has anyone seen the pumpkin he won?"

The guests, no longer able to pretend they weren't eavesdropping, broke into denials and recriminations. Some of them pointed at each other and made accusations. Estelle listened with more patience than I possessed. My exhaustion had kicked in again, and I found myself instinctively leaning closer to Xavier. A Reaper wasn't usually the biggest source of warmth, but the cold night air cut at my bare skin and made me want to bury myself in his arms until the outside world went away. A week of his absence had felt like a lifetime.

The dead body, however, was difficult to ignore, even if its former occupant was gone.

Xavier briefly drew me to his side and then crouched beside the inert form. "He was strangled, I think."

"Yeah... Estelle and I thought someone strangled him with his own costume." He couldn't have done it to himself, surely. "Xavier, should you still be here? Or will your boss be looking for you?"

I wanted him to stay, but now that the man's soul had gone to the afterworld, I was acutely aware of the possibility of his boss showing up and berating both of us. In the eyes of the Grim Reaper, anything that didn't involve Reaping the souls of the dead was an unnecessary distraction. Xavier and I had worked on disabusing him of that notion, but that had been before the recent incident that had sent us spiralling back to square one.

"He might," Xavier said, "but someone needs to tell Edwin… Oh, he's here."

The crowd's voices died down a little when Edwin came walking into view. The elf was hardly an imposing figure, but the two huge trolls who flanked him made everyone think twice about making trouble. From how short a time it'd taken him to get here, I'd guessed correctly that he'd been at the police station instead of the party. The poor guy rarely seemed to take any time off.

Xavier glided forward to meet him. "This man was murdered… strangled, I think."

"Who found the body?" Edwin's attention landed on me, and I gave him a look that communicated, *Hey, it wasn't me this time.*

The man in the eyeball mask stepped forward. "I did. I was walking home, and I nearly tripped over him. He must have left the party just before I did."

"Is that so?" asked Edwin. "I think you'd better come with me."

"I didn't do anything." The eyeballs on his mask bounced up and down in his agitation. "I was just walking home."

"Really." Edwin turned to the unruly guests who'd gathered in the mouth of the street. "Hasn't anyone called the hospital?"

"I did," Estelle said apologetically. "They should be here soon."

"Good." To the crowd, he said, "Go on... back to the library."

Estelle repeated his words, but without her microphone, she didn't quite command the same authority, and the crowd's curiosity refused to be suppressed. Some left, but most lingered, watching Edwin as his trolls herded the eyeball-masked man down the side street towards the police station. Part of me wanted to follow—it might not be any of my business, but the man *had* been at our party when he'd died—but I couldn't bring myself to leave Xavier's side.

"You should go," he whispered to me. "Back to the library."

"I know, but..." The man who'd died had been at the party, so the odds were high that the murderer had been among the guests too. *Are they still there?*

I looked at Estelle, who was talking to a couple of young women dressed in slinky cat costumes, and then whispered to Xavier, "How long ago did he die, do you know? Might his killer be nearby?"

"Not long before I was drawn to collect his soul," he murmured. "I doubt the killer would have returned to the library, though, if that's what's worrying you. It'd be too conspicuous."

He knew me too well. "I wish there was something we could do."

"That's enough." Edwin was back, his troll guards in tow. "All of you go home and stop staring. Except you, Estelle."

Her shoulders stiffened. "Me?"

"As you're the host, I'd like to talk to you about the events leading up to this incident."

Someone's not pleased to have missed out on the party. "Xavier has relevant information too," I told him. "He's the one who collected the man's soul."

Edwin sucked in a breath. "Fine."

He turned away and marched down the side street. Probably, he didn't want to stand outside arguing in the cold, which was understandable, and the growing sound of sirens on the seafront indicated the town's team of medical wizards were close at hand.

"He's definitely not pleased at being stuck at the office while everyone was dancing," I murmured to Xavier as we walked after Edwin. "Ah... sorry. I know you wanted to come too."

"It's fine." He flashed me a half smile. "I don't mind missing the party. There'll be others."

But will you be allowed to come? The question lingered in my mind as we walked past the clock tower, onto the wider street facing the seafront. The tide was in, sweeping around the pier that jutted outward into the ocean, and the breeze was even stronger without the surrounding buildings as a buffer.

Teeth chattering, I leaned closer to Xavier and wished I'd brought my cloak. Wait, I did have my wand. Shaking my head at the lapse of common sense, I paused outside the police station to cast a conjuring spell.

"Good plan," Estelle said as I draped the cloak around my shoulders. "You know, the other guests had some interesting things to say about Calvin—the murder victim, I mean."

"Like what?" I waited as she raised her wand and conjured up her own identical blue cloak, which she wrapped around herself too.

"According to several people, Calvin just inherited a fortune," Estelle confided in us. "A pretty substantial one."

"From relatives?" Was that why people had been irked

when he also won Estelle's contest too? "I guess we should probably tell Edwin that."

"Exactly."

She walked ahead of us into the police station, which contained a simply laid-out office room with a desk and not much else except a few doors that led to smaller interrogation rooms. At the back was another door, on the other side of which were the holding cells and the prison itself. Like a lot of small magical communities, Ivory Beach's resources were pretty limited. There was a reason Evangeline frequently locked up rogue vampires in the dungeon of her home instead.

The eyeball-masked guy was already inside one of the questioning rooms, closely watched by one of Edwin's security trolls. Edwin walked in, while Estelle and I took that as permission to follow. Xavier did, too, his Reaper-like tendency to blend into shadows making him appear to take up less space than the average person.

"I want you to tell me what happened," Edwin said. "No more, no less."

Terrance gave his account again of finding the body. He still hadn't removed his eyeball mask, which didn't help my doubts about his own involvement in the situation. For an innocent man, he sure didn't act like it, but nobody expected to trip over a dead body on the way home from a party.

"After he told us he'd found the body, we came with him to check the man was dead, in case he was mistaken," Estelle added. "We reached the body, and then Xavier…"

"He Reaped the man's soul," I finished, hoping Edwin didn't ask for details. I'd seen more than any regular human should have been able to, thanks to the unusual nature of my relationship with Xavier, but that didn't mean I wanted to say so in front of a guy who might or might not be a murderer and wore a mask covered in dangling eyeballs.

"Is that it?" Edwin enquired. "Why were all those people outside?"

"Some of the other guests from the party got curious and followed me," Estelle explained. "Though… they told me a few things about the murder victim that might be relevant."

"Such as…?" Edwin invited.

Estelle shuffled from one foot to the other, notably uncomfortable. "I thought you should know that a few people told me that he recently inherited a lot of money, which might point to a motive for his death."

"I'll be the judge of that." Edwin addressed Terrance next. "Were you aware of this?"

"Yes, everyone was," he mumbled. "I didn't know him that well, though. It's just what I heard from people who came into the shop where I work."

Edwin turned towards us. "Estelle, did these talkative guests happen to mention the unfortunate victim's employer?"

"Someone said he was an independent contractor," she said. "Not sure what industry."

"Construction," said Terrance. As if realising he'd answered too quickly, he added, "Ah, I don't know anything else, though. Honest." The eyeballs on his mask swung back and forth in his agitation.

"Please take off that mask," said Edwin with a touch of weariness. "It's not helping."

"A few people also mentioned a business partner," said Estelle with a touch of apology in her voice. "You might want to talk to some of the guests."

"Was this business partner at the party?"

"Er…"

Good question. If Edwin and the trolls opted to come back to the library and search, that'd bring a sour end to the festivities, but so would a killer being on the loose in my family's home.

I looked at Estelle and saw my own indecision reflected back at me, but she said, "I would assume so, but a lot of the guests have already left."

A muscle ticked in Edwin's jaw, as if he'd picked up on the unsaid implication that she'd made that assumption because most of the town had been at the party. "Is there anything else I should know?"

"He won a prize tonight," Estelle said. "Calvin did, but it's gone missing. I did wonder if the murderer might have taken it, but I mean… a toy pumpkin isn't worth murdering someone over."

"A toy pumpkin?" Edwin repeated dubiously. "I shall ask some questions, but I think that's enough from you and your cousin. I'll see you at the library later."

As I turned to leave, I glimpsed Xavier stepping out of the front door ahead of me and hastened to catch up to him. "Are you going back home?"

"I should, before my boss starts looking for me," he said. "I'm sorry, Rory. I don't want to risk his ire by staying out later than I need to."

My heart seized, while my head swam with questions. Why had he been late to collect the victim's soul? Had the Grim Reaper—no, he hadn't forbidden us from talking to one another again, surely, but I'd hardly seen him in over a week. Besides, Xavier was usually the voice of reason in these situations.

"You don't think… I mean, I heard Evangeline was out of town tonight," I began, half out of a desire for him to stay and half curious to know if the vampires had been involved in whatever had delayed his arrival in collecting the man's soul.

"No," he said. "It wasn't the vampires. I'm sure. He was definitely dead."

"Right." If he'd been bitten, he'd have fallen into a vampire coma, and Xavier wouldn't have been able to collect his soul.

"It's all right, Rory," he said. "I'm sure it's a one-off. Nothing involving…"

The Founders, I mentally filled in the blank. Yes, it was possible someone had been out to make trouble even without the vampires present, but old instincts were hard to suppress.

As I opened my mouth to reply, a shadow fell over the path alongside the seafront. My heart gave an uneasy swoop when a hooded figure loomed over both of us, even taller and grimmer than his apprentice.

"Erm. Hi." Not the best way to address the Grim Reaper, but it was about all I was capable of when faced with his intimidating presence.

"You." His voice was an echo in a vast canyon, calculated to make me feel as small and insignificant as possible. "I told you not to call my apprentice away."

"He came to collect a dead man's soul." I raised my head to meet the spot where his eyes should have been. "Besides, you *told* me and Xavier that we have permission to… to date one another."

Now wasn't the time for this conversation, but he'd been intentionally keeping Xavier away from me for over a week, and the blatant unfairness was too much to ignore.

"That was before you broke the terms of our deal. Come, Xavier."

The Grim Reaper swept out a hand like a raven's wing, enveloping his apprentice, and both vanished into a shadow as black as night.

"We didn't break our deal," I muttered ineffectively.

Estelle caught my arm and gave it a reassuring squeeze. "He'll get over it. This is probably a busy night for him."

"Yeah. You're right." It would be unfair to focus on my

own problems when her party had just blown up in a major way, so I forced my attention back to the present. "We should let the guests know the show's over."

"Before the police show up," she agreed. "Good call. It's better to do it on our own terms."

Edwin had other ideas, and we'd barely got halfway across the square before he came hurrying after us. He wore the usual long-suffering expression he reserved for dealing with my family, which said something along the lines of "Why is it always you?" That was accurate but not necessarily fair because of the sheer number of people who'd been at the party. Not to mention it was Halloween, the one night of the year that he could pretty much guarantee running into some kind of magical troublemaker. Why else had he been at the office in the first place?

"I have the name of the victim's business partner," he told us. "Terrance was certain he was at the party. May I come into the library?"

"I... Fine, but can I tell the guests to leave first?" Estelle asked.

"Go ahead." He waited expectantly while one of his troll guards came lumbering out of the side street to join him.

And with that, the party was officially over.

4

"Believe it or not, this isn't the worst end to a Halloween party I've been to," Aunt Candace whispered loudly as we watched Edwin's trolls dismantling the party with the efficiency of rampaging manticores. "I once went to a rave where the host ate three of his guests."

I ignored her, not in the mood for her tall tales. Poor Estelle had barely had time to grab a microphone and announce the library was closing for the night before the police had come marching in, and she'd had to stop to swiftly turn the lights on before they accidentally knocked all the furniture over in the darkness. The music cut out, too, leaving the bewildered guests marooned on the dance floor or scattered around the lobby.

"Everyone downstairs!" Edwin called out. "I want all the guests to assemble here in front of the doors immediately."

That might be asking for too much. While the upper floors were off limits, the guests had scattered all over the lower level and had vanished into all kinds of corners and crannies. Estelle unearthed a pile of werewolves sleeping behind a bookshelf, while a confused wizard dressed as a pirate had somehow locked himself inside a cabinet. Together, my family members moved through the ground floor, rescuing people, while Edwin's trolls blundered around, herding people towards the centre of the room.

In the end, there were about fifty guests remaining. Most of the partygoers' costumes looked somewhat worse for wear by this point, including Aunt Candace, who wasn't even trying to hide her interest in the proceedings. Her pen and notebook bobbed up and down at her side as she watched the crowd from underneath her ghastly skin-covered mask. The bandages she'd draped herself in had started to unravel and were in danger of slipping off altogether.

"Everyone over here!" Aunt Adelaide, too, looked somewhat bedraggled, her costume's feathers drooping from her shoulders.

"What's going on?" several people called out. "Why is the party over already?"

"Someone is dead," Edwin announced. "Calvin Honeywood. Is Dwight Keaton here?"

A murmur passed among the crowd. Then a wizard wearing a cat costume came shuffling forward from among the guests thronging the lobby. From the way he swayed on his feet, I knew he was incredibly drunk.

"What's that?" he slurred.

"Calvin Honeywood is dead," said Edwin. "I'm told you two used to be business partners."

"What?" The wizard lifted his cat mask to expose bloodshot eyes and a nest of messy black hair. "He can't be dead. I just saw him."

"He was murdered," Edwin clarified. "You worked together, correct?"

"Used to." He looked around at the suddenly garishly bright lobby, some of the haziness vanishing from his face. "You're serious, aren't you?"

"Yes," Edwin said. "Did you see Calvin tonight?"

"I saw them arguing," said one of the werewolves we'd found sleeping in the corner. "Before the party started."

"What?" The cat-wizard gave him a disgruntled scowl. "That doesn't mean anything."

"But you did have an argument?" asked Edwin. "I think you should come with me, Dwight."

The cat-wizard didn't move. "I've been here the whole time."

"Can anyone testify to that?" He looked at the other guests, most of whom either shrugged or whispered to one another. Probably, it'd been too dark for most of them to see who else was present, and the fact that everyone had been wearing masks wouldn't have helped either.

"I saw Dwight leave the party and come back," someone said. "Or someone in a cat costume did."

"That's about twenty people!" said Dwight. "I'm not the only person dressed as a cat. I haven't been anywhere. Honest."

"We'll see," Edwin said. "Come with me."

"This is unfair," the cat-wizard griped when the trolls escorted him off the dance floor. "Calvin's whole *family* is angry with him. I bet one of them was waiting to ambush him on the way home."

More whispers broke out amidst the crowd, but Edwin ignored them. "Take him back to the police station."

Dwight looked like he might object, but the trolls' menacing presence put an end to any thoughts he might have had of fleeing, and he stumbled away with the careful dignity of the incredibly inebriated. If he had argued with his former business partner tonight, that did make him the obvious person for Edwin to question, but it was anyone's guess as to whether he'd be able to give any straight answers.

Several of the other guests followed in Dwight's lead,

while others began trickling out of the library too. Some stopped to compliment Estelle on the festivities, not seeming to mind the unceremonious end to the night. The majority still wore their masks, which made it hard to recognise who was who, and I didn't envy Edwin for having to disentangle a murderer from their number.

"Edwin's going to have a tough time," Laney remarked from beside me, as though she'd read my mind… which, since she was a vampire, wasn't far from the realm of possibility. "Did you speak to Xavier? I saw him before I went back into the library."

"Not much." I spoke in an undertone. "His boss showed up and reprimanded me for keeping him away from his duty. Even though he was, you know, Reaping someone's soul."

"Isn't this supposed to be a busy night for Reapers?" she said. "I bet that's why the boss was in a mood."

"Yeah." Chills broke out on my arms. "Might this have happened because it was… you know, Halloween?"

"I doubt it," Estelle said after overhearing. "Xavier or his boss would have known if something was amiss here, wouldn't they?"

"Yeah." That was true. Far more likely was that someone had taken advantage of half the town being at the same party. "It sounds like that Calvin guy had enemies."

"Yeah," Laney agreed. "What was that Dwight said? That his family were mad at him or something?"

"I don't know." Estelle's expression clouded. "I think Edwin wants to start by talking to Calvin's former business partner before anything else. Friendships can turn sour easily, especially when there's jealousy involved."

"Because he inherited all that money?" The cat-wizard hadn't denied their argument, but his drunken state would make it difficult for Edwin to judge his guilt.

"Come on. Wake up." Aunt Adelaide's voice drifted over

the bookshelves as she presumably talked to a sleeping guest. "Everyone has to leave. The library is closed."

We moved to help with turfing out any stragglers. After we'd poked in corners and alcoves to unearth the last of the guests, Estelle pulled out her wand and began cleaning up the newly vacated lobby.

"You don't have to do that now," Aunt Adelaide told her. "We can clean up in the morning."

"I don't want to come downstairs to this mess in the morning." She gestured to the spilled drinks and furniture that the trolls had accidentally knocked over. "Besides, Cass is still stuck upstairs."

"Oops." She'd have words to say about the current situation, I had no doubt, but my remaining energy was swiftly fading, and it was all I could do to keep my eyes open while I helped my family with the clean-up. No help came from Cass's direction or Sylvester's, either, but he probably thought he'd done his part by popping the pumpkin balloon at the right moment.

Luckily, Laney was in her element at this hour, and she worked hard enough for three people as she glided around the lobby, moving furniture and stripping away decorations. When she shoved a huge shelf aside with the strength of a weightlifter, she revealed Aunt Candace lurking in a corner.

"Hey!" Aunt Candace objected. "I was napping."

"That mask is hideous," Laney remarked to her.

"My thanks." Aunt Candace neatly stepped behind another shelf to hide herself from view.

"Hey, you don't get out of helping." I followed, grimacing when I saw most of her outfit had unravelled and left entirely too much skin on display. "You might want to fix your costume."

"That owl." Aunt Candace spun around, and Sylvester

shuffled into view with a piece of bandage sticking out of his mouth.

"I couldn't resist," he said in a muffled voice.

"Scoundrel." Aunt Candace conjured up a sheet with a wave of her wand and draped it around her body, but she still didn't remove her mask. "Did you enjoy the party, Sylvester?"

"It was exquisite," the owl deadpanned. "Didn't your sister tell you not to wear that cursed mask?"

"It is *not* cursed," she said haughtily. "And it is in no way to blame for how tonight turned out."

She spoke with such conviction that I was instantly suspicious. "Sylvester… what do you mean by 'cursed'?"

"The obvious." Cass appeared on the first-floor balcony and gave a round of exaggerated applause. "Well done on cursing someone to death, Aunt Candace."

"Cass!" Aunt Adelaide snapped. "That's uncalled for. And, Sylvester, you aren't helping."

Sylvester took flight with a loud, hooting cackle, bandages trailing from his mouth.

Cass's eyes narrowed a fraction when she saw Laney standing beside me. "What? It's true, isn't it?"

Without waiting for a reply, she sauntered over to the stairs and began her descent from the upper floor.

"Is it?" I addressed the question to Aunt Adelaide, who was usually the expert on this kind of thing. "I mean, it wouldn't be the first time a curse killed someone in the library, would it?"

"She's just trying to stir up trouble," Aunt Adelaide said wearily. "We'll look into it later when we've had some sleep."

"No, we won't," Aunt Candace interjected. "There's no curse. You aren't to lay a finger on my mask."

"The last time you wore that mask, half the first floor collapsed and nearly crushed us all to death." Cass reached the bottom of the stairs, though she made no effort to help with the clean-up. "I haven't forgotten."

"You just want an excuse to blame me for anything that goes wrong," Aunt Candace accused. "I won't listen to any more of this."

She marched away with her nose in the air, her pen and notebook bobbing behind her.

Cass rolled her eyes. "Didn't anyone warn her not to wear that mask?"

"I tried," Aunt Adelaide said with an edge to her voice. "I told you we aren't discussing this now."

While she resumed cleaning up the lower floor, I walked over to Cass's side. "Do you really believe Aunt Candace's mask was behind that guy's death? Or are you just trying to wind her up?"

"Yes and yes," she said unhelpfully. "We got lucky, really. Nobody hid the body *in* the library this time."

"You really think it was a curse from your aunt's mask that killed that guy, not premeditated murder?" Laney eyed her in surprise. "I didn't take you for the superstitious sort."

A faint flush rose to Cass's face. "It's not superstition. If you'd spent enough time in the magical world, you'd know that."

Laney merely blinked, unfazed. "No need for that. I was just curious, since it sounds like a bunch of people had good reason to be mad at the guy. He recently inherited a fortune and won a raffle that a bunch of people wanted to win. Isn't that more likely than a curse that might or might not exist?"

"Did you read anything from the guests' minds?" I'd momentarily forgotten that obvious advantage of hers. "Like that Dwight?"

Cass gave her a sharp look, but Laney shook her head. "His thoughts were muddled, and there were too many people around."

"You read our guests' minds?" Cass's voice gained a distinctly disapproving note. "Really?"

"Only because someone *died*." Laney's mouth curved into a frown. "I didn't read *your* mind, as well you know."

Cass wore a pendant designed to stop mind-reading precisely to stop her privacy from being violated. Laney had made it clear that she'd respect her boundaries, but Cass had flat-out refused to believe her. I'd hoped that the anti-mind-reading spell would stop her from constantly trying to pick fights with Laney, but while the pair hadn't been *quite* as argumentative as they had before Laney fell into a coma, their brief closeness had evaporated too.

That was the part I didn't get. I'd seen Cass spend hours sitting at Laney's bedside, reading to her as she lay unresponsive. That seemed to indicate more than a passing interest in her well-being, but now Laney was awake, they were back to feigned hostility. And it *was* feigned, I was sure, though I didn't have the faintest idea why. I was no use at figuring out people, even if one was an antisocial, animal-loving witch and the other a party-loving newly created vampire.

Estelle approached us, breaking the tension. "What're you all doing over here?"

"Discussing Aunt Candace's cursed mask," I said, mostly to take the attention off Laney's admission to mind reading. "Or Cass says it's cursed, anyway, and that it killed Calvin."

"Cass, that's horrible." Estelle's eyes welled up, and I wished I hadn't said anything at all. "And untrue. Of course Aunt Candace didn't have anything to do with his death."

"The curse probably got him on the way home," Cass went on. "Curses can act through people, can't they? So even if he had a bunch of enemies, it might have pushed one of them into acting against him."

"That's ridiculous." I moved closer to Estelle, glaring at Cass. "Drop it."

Cass shrugged. "I just meant that curses can cause people to do things they wouldn't usually do. Or act on impulses."

"So does alcohol, and there was plenty of that flying around as well," Laney retorted. "I don't buy it."

Neither did I, though I'd freely admit that my own education on curses was still in its beginning stages compared to most of the magical world. There probably *were* some curses that could cause people to commit murder, but I didn't want Estelle to feel even worse about the outcome of the night than she already did. Perhaps sensing she'd gone too far, Cass gave a shrug and walked off towards the living quarters without another word.

"Maybe we should have invited her to the party," Laney muttered. "If she feels that left out."

"She knows she didn't need an invitation," Estelle said thickly, her eyes glimmering with tears. "I think she's upset that the library's safety was compromised. She warned me enough times, but I…"

"I know." I reached over and hugged her. "I know you wanted the night to go well. Cass has no right to make you feel guilty for this. Or Aunt Candace."

"When she's upset, she thinks everyone else should be too," said Laney. "I don't need to be able to read her mind to figure out that one."

"Don't tell her that," I said. "She'll rip your head off."

Laney exposed her fangs, her grin back. "She can try."

"Ignore her, Estelle," I added. "She'll get over it."

She gave me a watery smile. "I'm well practised at that. Don't worry."

"Want me to put one of Sylvester's mice in her bed?" Laney offered. "She won't even know I'm there."

"Please don't." Estelle rubbed her eyes on the back of her hand. "I don't want any feuds. We'll just get this place back to normal and then go to sleep."

"Sounds like a plan." We'd already returned the furniture to its former state, but there were bits of crinkled paper from Sylvester's confetti all over the place, and I expected we'd be pulling fake cobwebs off our clothes for the next week.

Speaking of pumpkins...

"Did either of you find that toy pumpkin?" I asked. "Calvin's prize? It's not in the library?"

"No," Estelle said. "No, I can't find it anywhere. It's gone."

Had Calvin dropped it on his way home, or had someone stolen it before then? Or had the murderer snatched up the prize in an attempt to cover their tracks? Our questions remained unanswered, though a missing toy was far from the pertinent issue of the night.

Whether due to a cursed mask or a grudge, a man was dead, and he'd died close enough to the library that I had an inkling that the closure of the party itself wouldn't be the end of our involvement.

5

The library opened later than usual the next day, which was a relief to all of us, since we'd all been up far past midnight. The only person downstairs when I came down to breakfast was Sylvester, who greeted me with a cheery "Good morning to you!"

I side-eyed him. "What's got you in such a good mood?"

"What hasn't?" he asked. "You can't pretend you didn't have a fun night. You even got to see your Reaper."

"Because someone *died*." I didn't really need to say that bit, but the owl's nonchalance got under my skin—which was precisely the point, I assumed. "Does Aunt Adelaide really think Aunt Candace's mask is cursed?"

The mask had haunted my dreams the previous night, though Aunt Candace hadn't been wearing it. Instead, the scene I'd dreamt of had resembled one of the Founders' parties, and I'd been surrounded by other masked figures wielding blood-red cocktails. Despite all the times we'd thwarted them, the Founders would haunt my mind for a while yet.

When he didn't reply, I glanced at Sylvester. "I know you heard me."

"You also know the proper way to ask me questions."

"It wasn't that sort of question." Yes, I knew that the official way to get an answer to a specific question was to consult the appropriately named Book of Questions, which also happened to be Sylvester's domain. As the embodiment of the library's infinite trove of information—also known as a *genius loci*—he only allowed us each one question per day, so I didn't venture into the Forbidden Room unless I had an urgent query. This, as curious as I might be, wasn't urgent. "I was just making conversation, Sylvester."

"No, you were trying to get around the rules." He took flight, dropping feathers all over the kitchen table as he did so. "Nice try!"

I fished a feather out of a mug and poured some coffee out of the pot that Aunt Adelaide had left out earlier. "I wasn't trying to get around the rules."

My response went unheard, but I figured it wasn't worth wasting my day's question on a whim when I could just ask my family members for the details of Aunt Candace's mask. It certainly wasn't out of character for Aunt Candace to buy a cursed object or even put a curse on it herself as an experiment for novel research. Either way, I doubted the mask had been responsible for Calvin's death.

Estelle walked into the kitchen as I was finishing my coffee, yawning widely. "Hey, Rory."

"Hey." I gave her a smile. "I think your mum must have been downstairs earlier and left out breakfast, but I haven't seen her."

"I expect she's doing some last-minute cleaning up," she said around another yawn. "I'm still finding cobwebs in random places."

"That's how you know it was a good night." I spoke in a

light tone in an attempt to raise her spirits, not wanting to bring up the elephant in the room—or rather, the body in the alley—until she broached the subject herself. "We're not opening until noon, right?"

"Right." She nibbled on a piece of toast. "I think the library's taking objection to us rearranging the place yesterday. I keep finding books in random places as well as the cobwebs and confetti."

"They weren't moved by the guests, I hope."

"No, but I think we were a bit too vigilant with putting away any high-risk books from prying eyes. I found a volume of tongue-twister spells in my sock drawer earlier."

"Imagine what havoc people could have wrought with that, though." For my part, I'd stashed my dad's journal under the bed just in case. Luckily, it'd stayed put this time. Some of the library's penchant for moving things around was due to Sylvester or Cass playing pranks, but I'd made it clear that the journal was off-limits.

Aunt Candace made a brief appearance to grab coffee—thankfully without her creepy mask on—and vanished with the proclamation that she wasn't going to be roped into doing more cleaning. Probably, she was still annoyed at Cass's accusations the previous day, and she didn't linger long enough for me to ask any questions concerning her odd fashion choices.

Estelle's brief cheer dimmed when our aunt departed. "I'd better see if any returns have come in."

Sure enough, a new stack of returned books had accumulated beside the desk.

"I'll deal with those," I offered. "You should catch up on some sleep. You look exhausted."

"So do you," she retaliated. "You don't have to treat me like a glass ornament, Rory. I'm not that fragile."

"I never said you were." I stifled a yawn. "You did all the work yesterday, you know."

"Actually, I think Laney did most of the tidying up." She picked up the box of returns and began sorting the books into piles. "If anything, I'm better off working away from the public eye so people don't keep ambushing me to ask about last night."

"Why would they do that?" I joined her, picking up a thick leather-bound volume. "Nothing happened at the library. It's Edwin they'll need to ask if they want to know how the questioning is going, if they're really that curious to know."

"They'll probably still think I know more than they do." She gave a sigh. "I wish Edwin hadn't come into the library. If he hadn't, we might have avoided a public scene."

"I doubt most of the guests were sober enough for the police showing up to ruin the night," I reassured her. "Except Dwight. I wonder if Edwin kept him at the police station for long. Not to mention the poor guy who found the body."

"Terrance Lindon, was it?" She shook her head. "No, I doubt Edwin kept him there for long, unless he had reason to suspect that he was involved in Calvin's death. That ex-business partner, though… *he* didn't act innocent."

"That's true." Nobody would have been thrilled to be dragged away from a party to confess to murder, but if Dwight had done so, it would at least mean the case was closed and the library's involvement at an end. "Edwin will have had a long night. The guy's job is almost as joyless as the Grim Reaper's."

"I wouldn't go that far," she said, her mouth twitching into a smile. "Ah… Xavier…"

"I'll message him today." Why had I brought him up? "Hopefully, the Grim Reaper will have got over his sulk now Halloween's over."

I doubted it'd be that simple, but I was far too tired to

drag myself over to the cemetery, so I'd have to wait until Xavier was able to contact me. Our messages didn't always go through to one another, thanks to one of us living in a magical library and the other in the middle of the local cemetery, where there was usually no need to communicate with anyone—not with the living anyway.

To avoid the subject of Xavier, I went to return some books to the third floor. Even Cass had decided to sleep in, and the door to the Magical Creatures Division was sealed as tightly as the entrance to the fourth-floor corridor. Glad that there'd at least been no trouble from that direction the previous day, I put the books back into place and went down to fetch more.

By the time I'd finished putting all the returns back into their proper locations, the library was due to open, but not a single visitor walked in for the first hour. An air of tiredness hung over the library and probably extended to the whole town too. While I was in dire need of quiet after the previous night's excitement, Xavier's absence was an ache in my chest that refused to go away. At lunchtime, I decided to stretch my legs and sent a message to Xavier while I was crossing the square to the bakery.

Inside, Zee herself gave me a strained smile, glitter still clinging to her dark skin and her eyes shadowed with tiredness.

"Great party last night," she said. "Your family really knows how to put on a show."

"I'm glad you had fun," I said. "I'll tell Estelle. She could use some cheering up."

"Oh, is she upset about that man's death? Such a shame," she said, packing muffins into bags for us. "She really shouldn't blame herself. It's hardly her fault."

"I know, but she wanted the event to go without a hitch."

"Yeah." She finished packing up our lunches. "His family were my first customers today. The guy who died, I mean."

"What? You met his family?" I asked, disarmed.

"Yeah, they're a big deal, apparently," she said. "The Honeywoods are a semi-prominent coven who really think a lot of themselves. Or so their matriarch told me when she was ordering me to make breakfast for a dozen people. She told me the hotel's breakfast is subpar and that she wanted a refund if I didn't do better."

"Lovely." I wrinkled my nose. "The family's staying in town? They aren't from Ivory Beach?"

"No, and the sooner they leave, the better." She dropped her voice. "Last I saw, they were going to the police station, so poor Edwin is going to have a rough day."

"He had a difficult night too," I said. "Given that he was questioning Calvin's ex-business partner. Did Calvin's family mention anything about him?"

"No," she replied. "They didn't mention Calvin's job at all except that he's the reason they're in town. I gather there was something about an inheritance."

"He recently inherited a huge fortune, Estelle said." I figured that if she'd met his family, she'd know that much too. "Some of the party guests were talking about it."

"I heard a vague rumour, but I guess that explains why his family got here so quickly." When the door opened behind me, she dropped the subject. "I'll be sure to send anyone who's awake enough to the library to compliment your cousin, Rory."

"Thanks." I took the bag of muffins and nearly dropped it when I saw Xavier waiting for me in the doorway.

"Rory."

As we stepped outside, he wrapped me in a hug. Gripping the bag in one hand, I buried my head in his shoulder for a moment, as if we were the only people in the world.

"You got my message?" I mumbled into his shoulder. "Did the Grim Reaper let you out?"

"I won our latest argument." He took my face in his hand and kissed me gently. "Sorry I disappeared on you yesterday."

"It wasn't your fault." Bad timing aside, nobody held a grudge quite like the Grim Reaper. "You'd think he'd be a bit more understanding that you were actually doing your job."

"I'm not supposed to get involved in police investigations," he said. "I'm only around for the *collecting the person's soul* part."

"And you're not supposed to linger and talk to me either." I glanced towards the high street branching off the square that led to the town's cemetery. "How likely is it that he'll follow you?"

"He won't. He's busy." He slid his hand into mine, and we began to cross the deserted square.

"Not collecting anyone's souls, I hope."

"No, not that."

"Good." I probably didn't want to know what the Grim Reaper did with the rest of his free time, but I had to admit that I was still curious to know why Xavier had been late showing up to collect Calvin's soul yesterday. "I know Halloween is supposed to be busy for Reapers. There wasn't any trouble last night, was there?"

"Not here." His gaze flickered over to the high street, though not a shadow disturbed the bright, cold winter day. "Sorry, Rory. I'd tell you everything, but then my boss *would* show up, and I'm still rebuilding trust between us."

"I get it." It'd been worth a shot. Theoretically, Xavier wasn't meant to tell me any of the Reapers' secrets, and we'd already crossed enough lines just by dating one another. "Zee just told me that Calvin Honeywood's family showed up in town. You know, the murder victim."

"Oh?" He raised a brow. "They aren't local?"

"No, and they're leaders of the coven in whatever town they live in."

We reached the library, and I pushed open the door. The lobby was still empty of any visitors, and even though the furniture was back in place, the space seemed bigger and more deserted than usual, possibly due to the absence of the crowd that had filled the space the previous night.

"There aren't many visitors in here today. I think everyone's sleeping in."

"Except Calvin's family?" He waved at Estelle, who brightened when she saw the bag in my hands.

"Zee's bakery?" she said. "Excellent. I'll tell my mum. She's been busy checking all the rooms back there, and they're in a real mess."

"Sylvester?" I guessed.

"I don't think so," she replied. "He's never literally turned a room upside down before. Let alone three of them."

"Upside down?" Xavier looked at me questioningly.

"I didn't know that was a thing either." I was still learning my way around the library's numerous idiosyncrasies nearly a year after moving here.

"It happens." Estelle smiled when I handed her the bag from the bakery, after I'd fished out a couple of muffins for Xavier and me. "We had to do a lot of rearranging to stop the guests from going anywhere they shouldn't have, and I guess the library's still getting over the shock."

I left Estelle to take lunch to Aunt Adelaide and settled at the desk with Xavier, munching on muffins and watching the door. Since there were so few visitors, it was almost like we were alone together, an all too rare occurrence recently.

"You wouldn't think there'd been a party here last night," Xavier remarked, gesturing at the lobby. "You cleaned up fast."

"Laney did most of the work," I admitted. "She was wide awake when the rest of us were dying on our feet."

"That's right." Estelle was back, finishing off her muffin. "Do you two want to go out for a walk? I don't mind watching the desk."

"I think it's raining." Xavier indicated the window. "It's up to you, Rory."

"I think we'll stay put for now." Not least because the Grim Reaper was less likely to ambush us inside the library. I got out of the way of the desk and stumbled over a trapdoor that had appeared on the floor beneath my feet. "No, we don't want to visit the vampire's basement."

"Definitely not." Estelle eyed the trapdoor. "I haven't seen that for a while."

"Might have been stirred up by the library being unsettled." The mysteriously sleeping figure in the library's lower level was one of its many unsolved mysteries, and the room seemed to appear and disappear whenever it felt like it—or whenever Cass felt like pranking one of us.

Estelle sidestepped the trapdoor and moved behind the desk. She reached for the shelf underneath and then jumped when something squeaked at her. "What… Rory, I think your familiar is sleeping down here."

"Jet?" I peered behind her and spied my familiar lying on top of a stack of record books. "What are you doing in there?"

"It's too bright, partner!" he squeaked at me.

"I told you not to overdo it." I crouched down to better see the feathery lump that was my familiar. "Are you okay?"

"She told me to go to the police station today!" He hopped onto one leg and then fell over again. "Oh no! Oh no!"

"You mean Aunt Candace, don't you?" I held out a hand for him to jump onto. "What did she want you to do? Listen in while Edwin questioned the suspects?"

Typical. I usually tolerated her sending my familiar out to attend to her whims because it satisfied his urge to gossip while letting me sit and read in peace sometimes, but I'd have to have a stern word with her if she wanted him to spy on an active crime scene.

"Is that allowed?" Xavier asked dubiously.

"Probably not." I lifted my familiar up to my face. "Jet, you don't have to spy on anyone for her."

"She told me," he squeaked feebly. "It's very important, partner."

"I doubt it." I gave him a stroke. "Don't let her bully you."

"The pumpkin!" He gave a sudden agitated jump and nearly fell off my hand. "Partner, I saw the pumpkin!"

"What pumpkin?" *Wait.* "Not the pumpkin toy Calvin won in that contest?"

"Yes, partner!" he said. "I was going to tell you, but I fell asleep!"

"Tell me what?"

"Someone stole it!" he said.

"Is that why it never turned up?" I glanced at Estelle, whose eyes widened in surprise.

"Yes, partner!" He hopped into an upright position again. "I saw someone carrying the pumpkin toy out of the library! I remember that man dressed as a mummy won the prize, but it wasn't him."

"Not Calvin himself?" I asked. "Er… are you sure you weren't dreaming? When did this happen?"

"Before the end of the party!" he said. "When the party ended, I told Candace, and she said the police would want to know."

"Why? Because the person who stole it might have seen who killed Calvin?" Estelle asked. "Or—the murderer was the thief?"

"Sounds like it went missing before he even left the library," I added. "Jet, what did the person look like?"

"A fairy, partner!" he said.

"An actual fairy or someone dressed as one?" It'd been dark enough in the library that I'd have had trouble identifying anyone, and it was unsurprising when Jet shook his head.

"Couldn't tell, partner!"

"Well, it's a start." Might the person who'd stolen the prize have seen the killer, or were they the same person? Edwin might appreciate knowing—or not, since the report came from a crow and wasn't detailed enough to point towards the thief's actual identity.

"I can head to the police station," Xavier offered. "If Calvin's family is there, you might want to stay behind."

"No. I'll come with you. I think Edwin should know about this pumpkin thief."

"Are you sure?" Estelle asked. "You don't want to waste the time you have with Xavier hanging around at the police station, do you?"

"I don't mind." I tensed at the implication in her voice. "He and his boss came to an understanding."

"Right." Xavier's mouth turned down at the corners. "We're working on it."

"I hope so," said Estelle. "Really, you'd think he'd be over this by now. He's an ancient immortal who ought to be above things like petty jealousy."

"We must have hurt his feelings when we went behind his back." I rolled my eyes. "Also, if you see Aunt Candace, tell her it isn't cool to send my familiar to spy on the police."

"I'll definitely let her know that," she said. "Are you sure it'll be worth it, though? There were a bunch of people dressed as fairies, and Jet might not have seen them properly in the dark."

"I know." The thief might have just taken advantage of his distraction and not be linked to his death… but there was always that possibility. "I'd like to see what's going on with Calvin's family, though. Zee said they were a nightmare to deal with."

"I guess they did have some motive for being involved in his death," she acknowledged. "Let me know what Edwin says."

Xavier and I left the library and walked across the square towards the police station. The cold wind instantly got into every gap in my coat, but it blew away some of the stuffiness of being stuck indoors, and at least I had Xavier close at hand for warmth.

"I won't be able to stay for long," he told me. "I'll need to check in with my boss… but we can go to the Black Dog pub later, if you like."

"I'd love to." I smiled. "It's been forever since we've had a real date."

Having him come to stay at the library had been out of the question as well. For all my flippant remarks about hurting the Reaper's feelings, we'd crossed some crucial line when Xavier had given me a magical stone with the ability to call him directly to my side in times of need—without telling his boss. While said stone had saved my life, the Grim Reaper had seen his action as a violation not just of their mutual trust but also of the agreement we'd come to when Xavier and I had first been dating. I really didn't need for us to be sent spiralling back to square one, where I'd trod on eggshells and feared that one day the Grim Reaper would sweep Xavier out of town altogether.

Sensing my mood, Xavier squeezed my hand in his and gently kissed me on the lips. He was cold but not too cold, a reminder that he wasn't quite of this world. And by association, neither was I.

"It'll be fine," he said. "Believe me."

I was starting to have second thoughts about spending our valuable time at the police station instead of together, but we'd already reached the side street by the clock tower. When we neared the crime scene, Xavier stopped for a moment.

"What is it?" I didn't see anything out of place, but I lacked a Reaper's close insight into the afterworld. I did have some benefit, as the reason I was now able to see Xavier send people's souls to the afterlife in the first place was because being close to a Reaper gave me a front-row seat. Most people definitely wouldn't enjoy the experience, but anything that reaffirmed our closeness was a bonus in my book.

"Nothing," he said. "Just wanted to make sure there wasn't anything awry that I overlooked last night, but I don't think there is."

"All right." I heard raised voices from the direction of the police station. "That must be Calvin's family."

My second thoughts multiplied to third and fourth ones. Through the transparent automatic doors to the police station, I could see that the entire reception was full of blond-haired witches and wizards with a striking resemblance to their deceased relative and that they were all talking at full volume. I didn't even see Edwin among them, though I spied one of his hulking troll guards at the back.

The doors slid open, and a broad-shouldered witch with layers of gravity-defying blond hair stuck her head out. "No room in here! You'll have to come back later."

"Who's there?" Edwin's voice came from behind the desk, which he seemed to be using as a shield between himself and the witches and wizards that I could only assume were members of the Honeywood family. "Aurora. Good, you've come to help."

"I've... what?" I looked at Xavier in alarm, but he'd

retreated, too, his gaze fixed on a point somewhere in the distance.

"Sorry," he mouthed at me.

Then he vanished into shadow, leaving me alone on the doorstep with no remaining defence between myself and the Honeywood family.

6

Never had I envied Xavier's ability to disappear into the shadows more than I did in that moment.

Behind the towering mass of hair atop the head of who I could only assume was the Honeywood Coven's matriarch, I caught Edwin's eye. "I need to talk to the police —alone."

"Rory!" Estelle appeared in the doorway like a guardian angel, her eyes widening at the sight of the Honeywoods crowding the police station. "What's going on?"

"Another one!" The witch zeroed in on Estelle. "We don't have space for you in here. I'm trying to solve my foolish brother's murder."

I thought that was the police's job. Neither Estelle nor I said that aloud, though if she was the victim's brother, it might explain why she and the others had been so swift to arrive in town. If Calvin hadn't had children, I imagined his siblings would be close to the top of the list to receive the inheritance he'd reportedly got his hands on before his untimely demise.

"Your brother was Calvin Honeywood?" Estelle asked. "I work at the library—"

"It was your party, was it?" asked the witch. "Oh, you're one of those covenless Hawthorns, are you?"

She said "covenless" as though it was some kind of medical affliction.

"And you must be Cecilia Honeywood." Estelle stepped protectively to my side. "I'm Estelle. This is my cousin, Rory, and we have to talk to Edwin."

"If it's about Calvin, the rest of us deserve to know too," said the witch. "The selfish fool up and died without leaving us a thing."

"In here." Edwin beckoned us into one of the side rooms, and one of his security trolls lumbered into the way to prevent the Honeywoods from following us. Once he closed the door, he addressed Estelle. "You had information?"

"Only that we heard who might have stolen that toy Calvin won at the party," Estelle said hesitantly. "Someone spotted them leaving the party with it. They were dressed in a fairy costume."

"That's it?" His shoulders slumped. "You came all the way here to tell me that?"

"You looked like you needed rescuing," Estelle said in an undertone, though the strident noise of Cecilia Honeywood arguing with the security troll came from the other side of the door. "I heard the Honeywood family was in town, but they're even worse than the rumours."

"Did you follow me and Xavier?" I asked her, also dropping my voice to a whisper.

"I had a feeling," she muttered back. "I didn't trust Xavier's boss not to show up, and from what I've heard about the Honeywoods…"

Edwin cleared his throat. "While you're here, you might as well tell me what else you know."

"That's it." The clamour of voices outside the door made

it difficult to think clearly. "How'd the Honeywoods find out Calvin was dead?"

Edwin sighed. "I assume they tried to call him and someone from the hospital answered his phone. That's my understanding of the situation."

"What did Cecilia mean when she claimed he left them with nothing?" asked Estelle. "That's not what I heard."

"Don't ask me to explain their tangled dynamics," he said. "Besides, what am I supposed to do with that information you gave me? Ask for a list of people who were dressed as fairies?"

Some gratitude for rescuing him from the Honeywoods. Not that we'd be safe for long. An ominous silence from the lobby was followed by a loud knocking on the door.

"Are you done in there?" asked the blond witch. "I have more questions I need to ask the party's host."

"That's me." Estelle stepped forward resignedly. "I'm afraid the police are in charge of the murder investigation, so I don't know any more than you do about what happened to Calvin."

"Yes, we're in charge of the investigation," Edwin said pointedly. "Estelle, would you mind speaking to them and allaying their concerns? I think they'd appreciate an explanation of this contest Calvin won, for instance."

"What contest?" Cecilia zeroed in on Estelle. "Nobody mentioned a contest."

"It was a kind of… raffle that I held at the party," Estelle said. "Calvin won a toy pumpkin that disappeared. Ah, possibly stolen by one of the guests."

The Honeywoods crowded around Estelle and began asking questions. Edwin's obvious relief that they'd stopped badgering him prompted me to ask, "Are Terrance and Dwight still here, or did they go home?"

"I sent them home," he said. "I intended to call them in for questioning again, but—"

"But the Honeywood family showed up." From behind the door, I counted less than ten of them, fewer than I'd initially thought, but it was hard to keep track because they kept moving around, and Cecilia made enough noise for a dozen people.

"Right," she announced. "Now the party's organiser is here, we can figure out this mess. Come out here, Edwin."

You aren't escaping that easily, I thought as the elf's shoulders slumped. Poor Estelle was surrounded as the family members bombarded her with anecdotes and accusations, and I hadn't the heart to abandon her. Not that I could get to the front door with a coven standing in my way. Within two minutes, I was a reluctant expert on the situation. It swiftly became apparent that Calvin hadn't set up his own will and that everyone wanted a piece of the fortune Calvin had inherited from his father not a week before his death. Evidently, they thought micromanaging the murder investigation would get them to their objective.

"I can't believe he was so careless," Cecilia reprimanded Estelle. "You, as the host, should have been responsible for his safety."

"He wasn't murdered *at* the party," Estelle said, flushing. "Besides, it's hardly his fault."

"Oh, it's definitely his fault," said a blond wizard of around forty or so. "He thought he was invincible because Dad gave him everything when he died."

"It's ridiculous," added another blond witch in her early twenties. "Why did he do that? They weren't even close."

"I know," said Cecilia. "*I'm* his favourite child."

"Or so *you* say," said the blond man in a nasally voice. "I have more children than you do. And a bigger house. I need the money."

"Oh, don't be absurd," she said. "It's only bigger because you added an extension that you didn't even need."

They went on like this for a while, and I tried to sort out who was who. I gathered that three of the Honeywoods present were Calvin's siblings, while the younger members were grandchildren of the man whose initial death had kicked off this whole fiasco. The fact that the wizard in question had foisted his entire fortune upon someone who'd been murdered within a week pointed towards someone inside this very room being responsible, but I wasn't going to be the one to state the obvious. Surely Edwin had already realised that was the most likely outcome.

I might have identified Cecilia as the killer if not for the fact that she seemed to be intent on doing Edwin's job for him—unless she hadn't known what consequences Calvin's death would result in. Maybe she'd assumed he'd already assembled a will of his own to distribute the money to the rest of the family, but either way, I doubted we'd get very far by making an outright accusation. It'd take an entire army of trolls to get one of the Honeywoods into an interrogation room.

After exhausting the few answers to their questions she could give, Estelle began trying to make her way to the door. "I'm sorry for your trouble, but there's nothing more we can do for you."

I joined her in her attempts to extricate herself from the Honeywoods, but Cecilia hounded us to the door, flanked by her blond clones.

"You can't just leave!" she said. "We need justice."

"That's the police's job," Estelle said with firmness that was usually uncharacteristic of her. "Edwin's trying to help. Ask him any more questions you might have."

We edged out of the door and all but sprinted along the seafront, down the side street, and across the square. Breathless, we finally slowed at the library's doorstep, both of us relieved to see that the Honeywoods hadn't followed us.

"What a mess," Estelle said between gasps. "I forgot how petty some coven leaders can be, and Cecelia is worse than most I've met."

"I have a hard time imagining worse." I clutched at a stitch in my side. "It's safe to say Edwin's going to be occupied for a while."

"Part of me wonders if that was their intention," said Estelle. "To distract his attention from investigating the crime. But I don't know. They seem…"

"Authentically annoying, not faking it?" I suggested. "Yeah, I don't know. I wish they'd give Edwin some space. I don't know how he's supposed to catch the actual killer with them hanging around him, making constant demands."

Not that that was our problem to solve. A few more people had trickled into the library while we'd been gone, while Aunt Adelaide had taken over the front desk. Aunt Candace, and Cass, of course, were absent.

"You were gone a while," Aunt Adelaide said as we entered the lobby. "Did Edwin want to question you?"

"Not exactly," she replied. "We had to escape Calvin's family."

"Escape?"

"They're awful," I explained. "Trying to micromanage the investigation at every turn. They heard Estelle was running the party and decided to start interrogating her."

"Surely if they were related to the murder victim, Edwin should have been the one doing the questioning," said Aunt Adelaide. "Aren't they potential suspects?"

"You'd think, but he was outnumbered," said Estelle. "The Honeywoods are a semi-prominent coven, apparently, and Cecilia certainly acts like she's important. Also, they're from out of town, so I'm not sure they were even around when Calvin died."

"I can't say I've ever interacted with them before." Her brow crinkled. "They came from outside of the town for the sole purpose of aiding in a murder investigation?"

"Allegedly, Calvin inherited everything from his dad, and now they don't know who's going to get the money now he's dead," I explained. "That might be a motivating factor."

"Yeah, and Cecilia thinks it should be hers," said Estelle. "Who's been here anyway? Anyone who was at the party?"

"I expect so," Aunt Adelaide said. "Most of the town was at the library, except Edwin, of course."

And Xavier. I didn't have a clue where he'd gone, and I could only hope that the Grim Reaper wouldn't stick his scythe in the way of our date later that evening too.

"I know," said Estelle. "I was just wondering if any of them might have seen who stole the pumpkin toy that Calvin won. We didn't have much chance to talk to Edwin, but Jet claimed the thief was wearing a fairy costume."

"I can't say it's likely that the other guests will remember," said Aunt Adelaide. "But feel free to go ahead and ask them some questions."

With her permission, we went looking for the library's handful of visitors. A few sleepy-looking witches had gathered in the Reading Corner, while a long-haired wizard was asleep in the hammock nearby.

"Hey," I said awkwardly. "Were any of you at the party?"

A couple of the witches nodded.

"Great night, Estelle." The wizard gave her a thumbs-up from the hammock. "Hey—did Calvin Honeywood really get killed? Or did I dream it?"

"No, it's true." I seized on the chance to follow that line of questioning. "You knew him?"

"No." The wizard yawned widely. "Not really. Just heard the rumours."

"We were wondering if anyone saw who took his prize," Estelle said hesitantly. "You know, that toy pumpkin. It never showed up."

Some of the witches exchanged whispers of interest.

"I bet it was Frances," said one of them. "She wanted that toy."

"Was she wearing a fairy costume?" I asked.

"No, a piranha."

So much for that idea. Nobody seemed to have very strong memories of leaving the party the previous night, and even Calvin's fate hadn't left a strong impression on them.

"I don't remember anyone dressed as a piranha," Estelle murmured. "Not sure we're going to get any answers here."

I racked my brain for any more questions I might have had. "Ah, did any of you see Calvin leave the party?"

One of the witches looked up blearily. "What was he dressed as again?"

"A mummy," I replied.

"I think I saw him," the witch added slowly. "He left with that... What's his name? The guy dressed in a rabbit costume."

"Which guy?" Had Calvin not left the party alone? Admittedly, relying on the memory of someone who'd been drunk and when everyone had been in masks anyway might not give the most accurate impression, but if he *had* been with someone else when he left, it might point to another witness.

"No idea," said her companion. "Maybe you imagined it."

"I didn't," the witch insisted. "Harold Spicer. That's the one."

"All right." I mentally filed the name away. It might be a dead end, but Edwin was going to have his work cut out for him trying to question people with Calvin's entire family breathing down his neck, so it wasn't the worst idea to pick up a few clues from our patrons.

Not many other guests showed up at the library that day, though that was probably a good thing, considering. The library remained in an apparent state of agitation over the rearranging we'd done the previous day. Amongst other incidents, the contents of two entire sections on the first floor switched themselves with one another, Estelle nearly broke her arm falling through the vampire's trapdoor, and a volume of poetry turned itself inside out with Aunt Adelaide's fingers trapped inside it. I had to break out my Biblio-Witch Inventory and write down a brand-new word —*reverse*—to free my aunt from the trap.

I could only assume the library was throwing a protest at us for holding the party, but it'd never objected to any of our previous events. It was a relief when evening came around and Xavier hadn't cancelled our date.

Hoping the Grim Reaper would keep his distance that night, I answered the knock on the door with a smile. Xavier greeted me with a hug and a kiss that wiped out my frustrations of the day, for the time being, and I practically skipped out of the library with him.

We crossed the square through the rainy night then retreated from the drizzle into the warm cosiness of the Black Dog pub.

A high volume of noise greeted us. My gaze zeroed in on the corner, where Calvin's family occupied a large table. Upon closer inspection, it looked like they'd shoved two tables together and stolen several others' chairs in order to fit everyone in. My heart sank. *Oh no.*

Xavier, unbothered, sat down at our usual table. I did so, too, but we'd barely placed our orders when the corner's occupants noticed our presence.

"Oh, it's her from the library," Cecilia said. "Those Hawthorn witches are *strange*, aren't they?"

"Speak for yourself," I muttered so that only Xavier could hear me.

He squeezed my hand reassuringly under the table.

"Who is that man she's with?" Cecilia went on. "He's handsome but so *pale*. What's with those black clothes? He looks like he's on his way to a funeral."

I choked on a laugh and lifted the menu to cover my face. "Sorry, Xavier."

"She's not wrong," he murmured out of the corner of his mouth. "Want to go somewhere else?"

"Nah, we've already placed our orders."

Our food showed up, and I dug into my pasta with less enthusiasm than usual. Despite my best efforts, one ear remained open to the ongoing conversation in the corner. After the Honeywoods had loudly dissected both of our fashion choices, they returned to debating the investigation into Calvin's murder.

"Would you believe that police station has a closing time!" Cecilia said. "It's completely unacceptable."

As far as I knew, the police station didn't actually have a closing time, but I didn't blame Edwin for coming up with an excuse to send them packing. They'd been making it all but impossible for him to do his job and investigate the murder.

"I don't understand how they do things here," one of her companions agreed. "He doesn't seem to want our help at all."

I can't imagine why. I picked up enough from eavesdropping to learn that Edwin had tried to ask each of them questions concerning Calvin's death, but they hadn't let him get very far.

"You'd think they'd know the police don't usually involve

civilians in investigations," I murmured to Xavier. "I guess being head of a coven supposedly lends special privileges."

"I just know he faked the will," Cecilia fumed, cutting through Xavier's reply. "It's so convenient that any copies were lost!"

Her voice was starting to give me a headache. Since they appeared intent on staying there all night—which made sense, since it was the pub closest to the police station—we didn't stay beyond finishing our meals. It'd started raining in earnest while we were eating, and I pulled up my hood when we walked outside.

"Maybe Calvin strangled himself to get away from them," I said to Xavier as the door closed behind us. "I wouldn't blame him at this point."

"No." He wrapped an arm around me. "We might have to find another pub for the time being."

"Oh, no, I'm not letting them drive us out of our favourite place." I kissed him lightly, his warmth banishing the cold. "Besides, they won't be here forever."

"I hope Edwin puts his foot down and sends them packing," said Xavier. "Granted, if he suspects any of them might have been involved… Oh no."

Unbeknownst to either of us, the shadow of the Grim Reaper had emerged from within the general darkness of the seafront. *Not again.*

"I have a job for you, apprentice," the Grim Reaper said, his voice echoing in the night.

"Now?" Xavier asked, put out. "You promised I could take the evening off."

"Your job is more important."

The Grim Reaper closed in. Xavier flashed me a look of apology, and then he vanished like smoke.

So much for a nice date.

7

I walked back to the library alone. Luckily, no Honeywoods waited to ambush me on the way back, but a black cloud as dark as a Reaper's cloak hovered over my head as I walked through the rain.

I pushed open the door to the library and entered, dripping wet, as Laney walked blithely out of the living quarters.

"Hey." She eyed me in surprise. "I thought you were with Xavier."

"Blame the Grim Reaper," I said. "And blame Calvin's family."

"What did they do?"

"Took over the Black Dog pub." I pulled out my wand and cast a drying spell that removed the rainwater from my cloak and hair. "Amongst other things, they were dissecting our fashion choices in full view of everyone inside the pub. Edwin booted them out of the police station, so they planted themselves in the nearest place to make trouble."

"How obnoxious." She flashed her fangs in a scowl. "Want me to pay them a visit?"

"I wouldn't," I said. "They're already making Edwin's life a misery. The sooner they're out of town, the better."

"Why're they so intent on 'helping' the police?" she asked. "Got something to hide, have they?"

"That's one possibility, but that Cecilia seems to think she's the centre of the universe regardless of whether she's actually owed anything or not."

I gave her a rundown of everything she'd missed while she'd been sleeping, which was less than I'd first thought. It'd kind of been a slow day, with the obvious exception of the time Estelle and I had spent at the police station with Calvin's family.

"Definitely fishy," Laney said when I'd finished. "Them Honeywoods think they own the investigation, do they?"

"Pretty much," I said. "I can't tell how much of it is because they want the inheritance and how much might be a sign that one of them was responsible for his death."

"Sounds like that Cecilia wanted the inheritance before he bit the dust," she said. "I'd say she got one of her minions to commit the actual murder."

"She and the others weren't in town until this morning, though. They weren't at the party."

"So?" Laney asked. "They might have put a curse on him the last time they saw one another. He'd have had to go home to receive his inheritance, right? That would have given them ample opportunity to strike."

"That's true." Not for the first time, she'd impressed me with how quickly she'd identified the magical possibilities that might have caused his death. "I think Edwin must have considered that possibility, but he hasn't had much luck questioning them."

"I could always snoop and see what they're up to when nobody is around," she offered. "They won't see me."

"Tempting," I admitted, "but I'm not supposed to be

involved in the investigation, and unlike the Honeywoods, I know when Edwin doesn't want me around."

"Calvin died on his way home from our party, though, remember? How long before his family decide to come here to the library to search for clues?"

I shuddered. "Don't even." They'd already taken over my favourite pub, though, and I wouldn't put it past Cecilia to leave no stone unturned in her attempt to find answers. "All right, but you might need earplugs when you're around Cecilia, especially with that oversensitive hearing of yours."

"Thanks for the warning." She grinned. "I already sleep with earplugs in, given that I can hear all the library's noise from upstairs during the day. And at night, I can hear your Aunt Candace snoring like a foghorn."

"Oh, fun." Another thought hit me. "Evangeline won't object to you sneaking around, will she? I know you haven't been going out as much..."

"It's not her business," she said. "Also, she said I could decide whether to come back to vampire lessons in my own time."

That was surprisingly generous of her, but none of us had expected Laney to make a quick recovery from her coma, Evangeline included. Compared to how the Grim Reaper was acting at the moment, the head of the local vampires and I had a positively cordial relationship.

"Good," I said. "Be careful out there, though, all right?"

"Always am." She flashed me a fanged grin and then vanished. The door closed behind her while I contemplated a less pleasant end to the night than I'd anticipated now that Xavier had gone.

Figuring I'd read a book instead, I walked into the living quarters... and then jumped violently. On the sofa sat a figure—no, not a figure, but a mask draped on the cushions in such a position that it looked as though someone was sitting there.

"Has Candace left that thing lying around again?" Aunt Adelaide walked into the room and picked up the horrible skin-like mask Aunt Candace had been wearing at the party.

"What did she do that for?"

"I haven't the faintest idea," she said. "Maybe it's the library moving things around again."

I grimaced at the way the bits of skin moved when she picked up the mask. "*Is* it cursed? What's the story there?"

"There's not much of one," she said. "Candace bought it from a market when we went to pick up a rare book from another town up the east coast. When she found out it was supposedly cursed, she decided she had to have it."

"So… you don't actually know if it's cursed?"

"It's certainly been the centre of a few incidents, but she refuses to take it to the curse breaker to check." She pursed her lips. "Perhaps I'll take it there tomorrow, assuming she hasn't noticed it's missing by then."

"Not so fast." Aunt Candace appeared in the doorway, casting a long shadow inside the already dimly lit living room. "I'll take that back, thanks."

She snatched the mask from her sister's hand and vanished with speed of which a Reaper would be proud.

Aunt Adelaide tutted. "Well, it was worth a try. Where's Xavier?"

I lowered my gaze. "The Grim Reaper swept him off again."

"Again?"

"Yeah." My heart flopped pathetically. "We were trying to escape the Honeywoods, but that wasn't what I wanted."

"I expect not," she said. "This isn't the first time you and the Grim Reaper have been through a rough stretch, is it?"

"No." That was the annoying part—I'd thought we were long past this. "The problem is that Xavier gave me that magical stone that allows me to call him to my side if I'm in danger without telling his boss. That's massively against the Reapers' rules, and when I used the stone at the Founders' house, the Grim Reaper saw it as a betrayal of our agreement."

"What kind of stone?" she asked. "I don't think you've ever shown me it up close before."

I fished the stone out of my pocket. Its smooth surface was unmarked, grey, and otherwise indistinguishable from any regular rock I might have stumbled over at the beach. Surprisingly, the Grim Reaper hadn't demanded that I give it back after the incident at the Founders' house.

Aunt Adelaide sucked in a breath. "Hmm. I gather the Reapers made it themselves? It's not like anything I've seen before."

"I assume they did, but you know how they are about sharing their secrets with outsiders."

"Yes… true." She peered at the stone's surface. "How do you use it?"

"Squeeze the stone, and it alerts Xavier to my location." Not that I'd needed to, in the end. He'd been able to track me through the afterworld, courtesy of the bond we shared, without the need to use any item to bind us. "Maybe returning it to the Grim Reaper will win me back into his favour, but he's never actually asked for it back."

"Might be worth considering," she said. "If you don't land yourself in trouble relating to the afterworld again. I really don't know how you managed to get yourself tangled with the one branch of magic that the library has little information on."

"Except the vampires?" I reminded her.

"Them too." She shook her head. "Sometimes I wonder if

my mother had the right idea. She rarely opened the library to the public outside of regular opening hours."

"Don't tell Estelle that." She loved using the library for social events, and being the host lit her up like nothing else. "Holding parties is her passion."

"Oh, I know, and I don't intend to stop her." She cast a glance up at the ceiling, as though she half expected it to collapse on her head. "Given the state of things, though, it might be wise to put any future events on hold."

Now I felt bad for Estelle, not just myself. Had the library truly been affected that badly by the event, or was there another reason it was acting out? Such as a cursed mask, for instance?

———

Aunt Candace must have got over her huff swiftly, because she showed up at breakfast the next day as though she'd never been angry at the rest of us at all. She joined Estelle and me at the table and began pouring out coffee. Sylvester flew in after her and landed atop the cupboard, watching us with his large owl eyes.

"Did you know they've examined the body?" Aunt Candace announced.

"What body?" Estelle asked around a yawn. We'd all had a somewhat disturbed night, as a batch of shelves on the first floor had collapsed into one another like dominoes for no apparent reason.

"Calvin Honeywood, obviously." She scooped a copious amount of jam onto her toast and took a bite.

"I didn't think you were interested," I said to her. "In his murder, I mean. You haven't asked any questions so far."

Not that I'd complain about her avoiding adding her

curiosity to the nonsense Edwin was already having to deal with thanks to the Honeywoods.

"That's because I've been dealing with judgement from you people over my personal possessions," she said through her mouthful.

"That cursed mask?" I guessed. "*Did* you put it on the sofa yesterday?"

"I did nothing of the sort." She took another bite. "Really, you'd think my sister would be more concerned with this crumbling ruin of a building than with my fashion choices."

Hearing a faint laugh from the cupboard, I lifted my gaze to Sylvester. "Do *you* know why everything is falling apart in here?"

The owl ruffled his feathers. "Need I remind you that there's a proper way to ask me questions?"

"It wasn't that sort of question." Giving up, I returned my attention to Aunt Candace. "What did they find out about Calvin's body, then?"

"That he was strangled."

"We already knew that."

"From behind," she added.

"With his own costume?" Estelle asked. "We knew that too. Unless they have some idea of who did it?"

"Who told you?" I asked Aunt Candace, suspicious. "You haven't had my familiar spying for you again?"

She sniffed. "Such accusations."

"He's inside your cloak, Aunt Candace," said Estelle.

Sure enough, Jet stuck his little head out of Aunt Candace's sleeve. "Hello, partner!"

"Have you forgotten he's technically *my* familiar?" Admittedly, I'd lost track of him after I'd left for my date with Xavier the previous night. I'd also forgotten to check in with Laney after she'd gone to spy on the Honeywoods, but she'd be asleep until dusk.

"There's no need to sound so accusatory. He *wanted* to help."

"You took advantage of him," I accused. "Anyway, why are you so interested in Calvin's death? Except for book research."

"Why else?" she said. "A man dies on Halloween, strangled by his own costume. The story writes itself."

As if to back up her point, her notebook and pen rose into the air at her side, the pen scribbling away on the page.

"Good for you," I said. "Did Jet happen to overhear anything else?"

"Oh, now you're interested." She grinned. "See? You're just as curious as I am."

"Not enough to buy cursed masks and…" I'd almost said *spy on people*, but hadn't I sent Laney to do the same?

"Did Adelaide tell you that story?" She rose to her feet. "She's terribly biased. You shouldn't pay her any attention."

She picked up another piece of toast and left the room eating it, Jet still perched inside her cloak.

Estelle poured more coffee. "I don't know why she thinks that mask is worth potentially cursing all of us. The novelty value, maybe."

"Might it have caused… you know, the weird incidents in here?" I glanced at Sylvester, a little put out by how swiftly he'd shot down my questions.

"I doubt it." She yawned. "Certainly not Calvin's murder. I wonder if Edwin ever got any peace yesterday."

"He told Cecilia and the others the police station was closed for the night," I said. "That's why they were at the pub yesterday evening."

"Sensible of him," she said. "If I were him, I'd stick to that rule as long as possible."

"I assume he hasn't had time to identify whoever stole that pumpkin toy, whether they were a fairy or just dressed as one." He'd hardly seemed to listen to us the previous day, but did I really blame him? "Or who left the party with Calvin. I know those witches yesterday mentioned someone dressed as a rabbit."

She finished her coffee. "Not sure we can take their word for it, to tell you the truth. Are there any reliable witnesses?"

"Not if everyone was drunk or too busy dancing." Except the people who hadn't attended the party in the first place. "Maybe we can drop in on Edwin before the Honeywoods show up again."

"He wasn't happy when we didn't have anything useful to share yesterday."

"Or…" I paused. "I can ask Laney. She went to eavesdrop on the Honeywoods last night."

"She didn't, did she?"

Sylvester gave a loud laugh, making both of us jump. "Really, it would save a lot of time if you just went straight to the hotel and turned the entire Honeywood family into cabbages."

"That wouldn't solve anything, Sylvester." Except Edwin's sanity, perhaps. Still, I figured it was worth seeing if Laney had heard anything worthwhile, so I left Sylvester laughing to himself in the kitchen and headed upstairs.

I had to knock three times before Laney answered her bedroom door. "Rory." She yawned, exposing her pointed incisors. "Oh. You want to know if I heard anything from Calvin's lovely family last night?"

"Did you?" I asked. "Sorry I woke you."

"I heard a lot about coven politics." She yawned again. "That Cecilia is her coven's leader, but I expect you already know that. She's furious that she didn't inherit anything from her dad despite being the authority in their community."

"Did she say anything to implicate herself in Calvin's death?"

"No," she replied. "She wants the investigation done. She also wants to take the inheritance without bothering with the paperwork, but that might be the best result for everyone involved."

"No kidding." What they expected Edwin to do about the missing inheritance was beyond me. "Thanks for helping out anyway."

I went downstairs to pass on her words to Estelle. "You know, it'd be convenient if one of the Honeywoods *was* involved in Calvin's death, but I guess it's too obvious. They also weren't at the party."

"Don't put that image in my head," Estelle said with a shudder. "I have a hard enough time thinking about that night without picturing Cecilia singing karaoke."

"Is it worth speaking to Edwin anyway?" I asked. "I know we don't really have any news… except the name of the person who supposedly left the party with Calvin."

"Harold Spicer," Estelle recalled. "Might be somewhere to start."

"Yeah." It was a long shot, I admitted, but anyone else who might have come forward with information would have run a mile as soon as they caught sight of the Honeywoods. "If we go to the police station now, Cecilia and the others might not have got there yet."

"I wouldn't count on it, but all right."

Estelle went to tell her mother where we were going and then joined me at the door. We walked out into another overcast day, huddling in our coats to keep out the cold November drizzle. With Halloween over, we were in that dismal period before the Christmas decorations went up and everyone started celebrating again. After Aunt Adelaide's comments the night before, I wasn't sure the library would be hosting any Christmas or New Year's parties, but I hoped she'd break the news to Estelle in a tactful manner.

At the suspiciously quiet seafront, we entered the police station, where a weary Edwin sat at the front desk. Mercifully, he was alone, though he groaned when he saw us. "Did you walk past the hotel? Now they'll know the place is open."

"It is open," I pointed out as the door closed behind us. "Have you been telling the Honeywoods the office is closed?"

The elf gave me a flat stare. "What else am I supposed to do? They won't let me do my job."

"Maybe the trolls should lock Cecilia in a cell for a while."

"I can't do that if she isn't a suspect. Besides, she's a coven leader, as she's told me a hundred times."

"That doesn't give her authority here," Estelle said. "Anyway, we have some possible useful information."

"Relevant this time?"

"Calvin left the party with someone, apparently," I said. "Harold... what was it? Spicer?"

"Did he, now?" Edwin pulled out his computer and began typing.

The sound of the door opening interrupted him, and Cecilia Honeywood sailed in with the air of someone returning from a voyage with riches beyond imagining. She brought an entourage of Honeywoods in her wake, all of whom filled the lobby as though Estelle and I didn't exist.

"We have so much to do today!" Cecilia declared. "Why— you look busy. What's that?"

My heart sank when she leaned over Edwin's shoulder and mouthed the name *Harold Spicer.*

"You didn't say you found a suspect!" she said.

"He isn't a suspect," Edwin said. "That said, he and the victim may have left the party together."

"That might not be true," I said quickly. "The witnesses weren't certain, and everyone at the party was in costume."

"Well, you'd better give him a call!" Cecilia insisted. "Or give us his address."

"You can't read that," Edwin told her. "That's private information."

"We must find him at once!" said Cecilia. "If this Harold Spicer saw Calvin before he died, we need to talk to him."

"That's not your job." Edwin wore an expression that put me in mind of a man contemplating the noose.

Sensing a temper tantrum brewing on Cecilia's behalf, I backed towards the door and straight into Xavier.

"Ah!" I jumped, startled, and steadied myself when he took my arm.

"Sorry," he said. "Good timing. You need rescuing?"

"I might." I glanced at Estelle, who was trying to extract herself from a web of Honeywoods. "What're you doing here?"

"Your aunt told me where to find you," he murmured. "I was going to apologise for last night, but I don't think it's a good time."

"It's *him*!" said Cecilia loudly, as though Xavier himself wasn't present. "The one with the strange fashion sense. Oh, did he know Calvin?"

"No," I said firmly, wondering how on earth she hadn't realised he was a Reaper. "We're going back to the library."

I took Estelle's hand to pull her out of the snare of Honeywoods, and the three of us escaped through the automatic doors.

"You know, I think Sylvester's idea to turn them into cabbages might have had merit after all," I remarked as we left the police station behind.

"He suggested that, did he?" Xavier fell into step with me, while Estelle walked on my other side. "Did Edwin have any updates?"

"No, and it looks like he'll spend the day stopping Cecilia

and the others from swarming this guy who may or may not have walked home from the party with Calvin."

"Harold Spicer," Estelle said. "I did get his contact details, for all the good it'll do."

"When did you do that?" She must have read over Edwin's shoulder while she'd been dodging the Honeywoods.

She flushed. "I know we aren't supposed to get involved in this, but I don't think Edwin's going to be able to pay any house visits without bringing a plague of Honeywoods."

I snorted. "You aren't wrong. You want to call that Harold guy in advance? Warn him in case they manage to wrangle his address out of Edwin?"

"That's what I thought," she said. "I don't know if it's the right thing to do, though, given that we're not the police."

"Neither is Cecilia," Xavier said. "If you like, Rory and I will come with you."

"Oh, I have his phone number," she said sheepishly. "I'll call him."

As she did so, I moved closer to Xavier and whispered, "What was the problem last night?"

"Nothing," he murmured back.

You mean nothing you can tell me about. My heart ached. I didn't want his secrets to put a wedge between us, but how could I ignore the way the Grim Reaper kept intentionally standing in our way?

"I'll tell you later," he added as Estelle spoke into the phone.

"Is this Harold Spicer?" she asked. "Yes… sorry to bother you. This is going to sound strange, but we heard a rumour that you left the party the other day with Calvin Honeywood."

There came the indistinct buzz of a voice on the other side while Estelle listened.

"Several witnesses said you did," Estelle went on. "Are you sure?"

Another pause and more words I couldn't hear followed.

"Oh, he was dressed as a mummy... all right." Estelle's shoulders slumped. "Thanks anyway."

She ended the call.

"No luck?" I guessed.

"His friend was dressed as a mummy, too, and they left the party together," she replied. "Easy mistake to make."

"Oh."

"He also didn't see Calvin," she added. "Maybe I should tell Edwin so he can make sure the Honeywoods stay away from someone who wasn't involved."

"I'll go," Xavier offered. "The Honeywoods are less likely to bother me."

"If you use your Reaper powers to materialise in the police station, it might shut Cecilia up for a minute," Estelle said. "Maybe don't do that, though."

"Definitely not." I turned to Xavier, my heart giving another painful twinge. "Do you have time to come to the library afterwards?"

"Not for long, but..." He glanced at Estelle, who'd turned away to give us some privacy. "Honestly, I don't know. The boss is being unpredictable at the moment. Something has him agitated."

"Such as...?"

"Halloween," he said. "Weird incidents involving Reapers. Not local but enough to grab his attention. I'd tell you more if I knew."

That was likely as much information as he was allowed to give me. "As long as he isn't policing you going on dates with me again."

"I did talk to him and made it clear where we stand," he

said. "Unfortunately, this time of year has him on edge. Give it a week, and he'll be back to his usual grouchy self."

"Not much of a change there." I hoped he was right. "Maybe he should blow off steam and terrorise Cecilia."

The mental image was entertaining, if nothing else, but to an immortal like the Grim Reaper, a grudge might well last forever. Would we ever be able to win him over again?

8

After Xavier departed, I had little choice but to go back to the library and wait for him to inform Edwin about the mistake with Harold Spicer.

I took over the front desk so Estelle could help her mother clean up the mess from a pile of collapsed bookshelves. Sylvester came to supervise me—or annoy me, same difference—and steadfastly refused to explain why the library kept suffering from minor disasters or collapses. Finally, when Xavier messaged me saying he wouldn't be able to come over until that evening after all, I gave in.

"I'm going to ask the Book of Questions to explain why the place is falling apart," I told Estelle. "Can you watch the desk?"

"Sylvester won't…?" She trailed off when Sylvester ruffled his feathers threateningly at her. "All right. I guess there's no point in asking the room to identify Calvin's murderer, so this is the next best thing."

"That's what I thought." Up until now, I'd resisted the impulse to ask the Book of Questions for any help with the investigation. Sylvester had made it clear that its knowledge only encompassed everything within the library itself. As the murder had taken place outside of it, the book would be no help in that scenario, but surely the book would be able to help us identify the source of the chaos inside the library itself. "Though we can't ask Edwin either until he shakes off the Honeywoods."

"No." She peered behind the desk. "Huh. The book isn't here. I could have sworn my mum brought it out of the back room after the party."

"I forgot you put it away." I ducked behind the desk myself to grab the key that worked on most of the library's doors. "Which room was it in?"

"Second on the left."

I crossed the lobby and veered off the Reading Corner to unlock the right door. When I pushed the door inward, I found an empty classroom on the other side that didn't contain a single book.

Assuming I'd picked the wrong room by mistake, I tried the next door but got the same result. After I'd peered into every room branching off the Reading Corner, I returned to the front desk.

"It's not there?" A worried furrow appeared in Estelle's brow. "I wonder if my mother moved it."

"I doubt she's had time." I looked pointedly at Sylvester. "Did you move the book somewhere?"

"You all tidied the place up," he said innocently. "Not me."

"Nice try." Yes, we'd tidied the library, because we hadn't wanted any members of the public to find the Book of Questions. Except in the process, we'd hidden it a little too well. I hadn't actually seen the book in days, since I'd been more fixated on putting my dad's journal in an out-of-reach place and I'd trusted the others to handle it. Sylvester, certainly, wouldn't have wanted random members of the public stumbling upon what he considered his most valuable possession.

Given his casual behaviour, I assumed he wasn't overly concerned about its whereabouts, which suggested it was still *in* the library… but where?

"I'll help you look around," Estelle offered. "Sylvester, can you watch the desk?"

"Yes, I can."

"*Will* you watch it?" I asked. "And not terrify the visitors?"

"So demanding." He clucked his beak. "Fine."

Relieved that he'd actually said yes, I walked to the Reading Corner again and showed Estelle the empty rooms.

"Weird." She eyed the classroom in puzzlement. "This is definitely the room I put it in."

"Has the library hidden it?" Was Sylvester messing with us after all?

"I don't know." Her brow creased. "It's not like the library to take away something that essential."

"It's happened before," I reminded her. "When it thinks the book is safer somewhere else or it feels threatened."

"It's been long enough since the party that the library can't possibly feel threatened."

"Has Aunt Candace seen it?" Or had her cursed mask played a part in its disappearance?

"She might have taken it for research," Estelle said dubiously. "She'll be in her room, I expect."

"I'll find her." I crossed the lobby to the living quarters and climbed the stairs to the top this time. I rapped on the door to the aptly named Research Cave with my knuckles. "Aunt Candace?"

"Enter at your own risk!" she said from the other side.

Bracing myself, I opened the door. Even my worst imaginings hadn't prepared me for the sight of her wearing the creepy skin mask and dancing around the centre of the room with her wand held aloft.

"What are you doing with that?" I backed out the door.

"I'm doing some method acting." She lowered her wand. "To get into the mind of a serial killer."

"I can see why a serial killer would wear that mask." I shuddered. "Is that mask the reason half the library is collapsing?"

"Don't be absurd," she said. "You're too superstitious. You people will believe anything."

"We live in a magical library with most of its knowledge contained in an owl."

"I am *not* an owl," Sylvester said loudly, making me jump. I hadn't seen him swoop in behind me. "And I might remind you that you're discussing eldritch secrets that could alter the very fabric of the universe. I could turn you into a pencil for a bit in case you want a reminder."

Uh-oh. "There's no need for that. I was just pointing out that it's a bit absurd for her to think a cursed object is super-stition. I haven't even lived here for a year, and I've seen dozens already."

"That's because you're a magnet for trouble," said Aunt Candace. "There's nothing wrong with my mask."

"Fine." I gave up. "I'm looking for the Book of Questions. Have you seen it?"

"Don't ask me," Aunt Candace said. "I haven't seen it since my sister locked it up before the party."

I'd have to take her word for it on that one. "I'll ask her."

Glad to turn my back, I left her with Sylvester, who didn't seem bothered by the creepy mask in the slightest. It'd take more than a little curse to faze the owl.

After I returned to the lobby, I followed the sound of crashing and swearing up to the second floor. Aunt Adelaide stood marooned in a sea of hardbacks that looked heavy enough to crush someone to death.

"The Dimensional Studies Section has folded in on itself," she told me distractedly. "I don't know what's going on, but fixing one shelf causes another to fall over. Is there something you need?"

"The Book of Questions has gone missing."

"Isn't it still in the back room?"

"No. I looked." I took a hasty step back when one of the remaining shelves began to buckle. "Estelle and I checked all the rooms, and Aunt Candace hasn't seen it either."

She swore and pointed her wand at the trembling shelf to steady it. "Maybe Cass has spotted it."

I'd run out of any other ideas, so I nodded. "All right. Also… Aunt Candace is wearing the mask. Might that be causing all this mayhem?"

"If it is, it's beyond me to stop her." She waved her wand to prevent another shelf from sliding sideways.

"Let me help." I reached into my pocket for my Biblio-Witch Inventory, which contained a compendium of all the words I'd learned to use to harness our family's magic. "Which spell should I try?"

Because of the confounding nature of the Dimensional Studies Section, stopping the destruction was beyond my skillset. I opened the Biblio-Witch Inventory, and the word *find* caught my eye, giving me an idea.

Could I use that spell to find the missing Book of Questions? Perhaps, but I put the thought out of mind for the time being and helped Aunt Adelaide return the shelves to their former state. It took several attempts to figure out which order to move the shelves in that wouldn't trigger another one to fall over. When that was done, there was just the matter of sorting the books out, but Aunt Adelaide insisted that I didn't have to help with that.

Before I left, I ran a fingertip down the list of words in my Biblio-Witch Inventory and tapped firmly on the word *find,* picturing the Book of Questions in my mind's eye.

The word glowed, but the book didn't appear. I tried again, with the same result.

"Rory, what are you doing?" asked Aunt Adelaide.

"I was trying to find the Book of Questions." I put my Biblio-Witch Inventory away. "Even a finding spell didn't work."

"That *is* strange," she said, worry clouding her expression. "It must be somewhere. Sylvester would have raised hell if it was really missing… or stolen."

"That's true." It was just like the owl to keep us in the dark, though there was still one person I hadn't asked yet. "Cass has been quiet lately. I'll talk to her."

"She's avoiding being asked to help clean up this mess, I imagine," Aunt Adelaide said. "Good luck."

I made for the stairs again, this time heading up to the third floor. As I reached the Magical Creatures Division, I remembered that there was one place in the library I hadn't checked on since the party: the fourth-floor corridor. The corridor comprised a hidden dimension created by my grandmother, and reality tended to get kind of… slippery up there. In fact, for all I knew, even my Biblio-Witch Inventory's finding spell would have trouble reaching anything on the other side. Perhaps that was where the Book of Questions had ended up, though I had a hard time believing Sylvester's contentious relationship with the corridor's guardian would so easily be erased.

An ominous growling greeted me when I opened the door to the Magical Creatures Division, and I found Cass crouched down beside the manticore's cage.

"What?" she shot at me. "Did you take my book of magical ailments?"

"Of course not," I said, taken aback at the accusation in her tone. "I was looking for the Book of Questions. It's gone missing, and my finding spell won't work. Might it be up on the fourth floor?"

"No idea. Why?"

"Doesn't it… bother you that it's missing?" I already regretted asking the question. "It seems to have moved of its own accord."

She grunted. "That's nothing new. Is Sylvester bothered?"

"Well, no, but he also thinks the destruction and chaos is a hilarious joke."

"It'll take more than a few glitches to unravel the library," she said. "Let me know if you find my book of magical ailments, won't you? The manticore has a cold, and I think it's contagious."

"Noted." I backed out into the doorway in case said cold was transmissible to humans. "Ah… have you gone into the fourth-floor corridor recently? Made any wishes?"

"No," she said. "There's nothing the room can give me that I can't get for myself."

"All right." I *hoped* she'd warn us before she conjured up a unicorn or something, but it sounded like her manticore had her full attention. The giant crab-lion thing was tetchy on a good day, let alone when sick.

After I closed the door to the Magical Creatures Division, I took in a deep breath and approached the entryway to the fourth floor. Unusually, the door was dark brown today. It was usually a much brighter colour, and the absence of its usual cheer brought me a sense of unease as much as the collapsing shelves did. If whatever was infecting the library had spread up here too…

Shoving the thought aside, I opened the door.

A shadowy form loomed on the other side, a solid block in front of me. I stumbled back with a gasp. While it only took me a heartbeat to recognise the corridor's guardian's transparency behind the shadows, that didn't make its presence any less alarming.

"What are you doing?" I backed up another step when the guardian advanced on me. "Don't scare me like that. It's just me. You know—Rory."

The guardian didn't reply, but I was pretty sure it couldn't actually talk. Being a living manifestation curse created by my grandmother to guard the corridor and prevent anyone who wasn't one of my family members from getting inside meant its methods of communication were limited, but the way it was intently driving me backwards was clear enough.

"I need to get upstairs," I went on. "I just need… the room."

The guardian remained in the doorway, unmoving, like a statue formed out of shadows. Kind of like the Grim Reaper, minus the scythe and the bad temper.

"What's the problem?" I tried to step forward again, but the guardian's presence solidified, pushing me back. This time, I tripped and fell on my rear with a thud. I lifted my head, and the door closed in my face.

What in the world?

The guardian hadn't chased me off since we'd first discovered the corridor and it'd assumed my family members and I were enemies or spies, not recognising us as relations of the person who'd created the upper floor in the first place. Namely, Grandma. Why would the corridor turn on me now?

I got to my feet and hesitantly turned towards the Magical Creatures Division, but a high-volume sneeze from the manticore warned me not to get too close.

I was halfway to the stairs when a crash rang up from the lobby followed by a scream. *Estelle.*

I broke into a run, taking the stairs two at a time until I reached the lower floor. The research section was in disarray. Numerous shelves had toppled like dominoes, as if someone had given them a massive shove from the front, and Estelle stood white-faced near the desk.

"Estelle!" I ran to her side. "Are you okay?"

"Yes." She gave a headshake, her eyes round. "They just… fell over. Did you see anyone from upstairs?"

"No… a person can't have done that."

Very luckily, there hadn't been anyone inside the Research Division at the time, but between that and the Dimensional Studies Section, we were resigned to spending the rest of the day putting shelves back up and picking books out of random corners. That gave me little chance to ponder on the reasons the guardian had shut me out of the upper floor, though I did tell Estelle about my unpleasant encounter.

"If you ask me, the guardian's trying to stop whatever's affecting the rest of the library from getting up there too," Estelle said as we were putting a collapsed cabinet back together. "We don't need this weirdness infecting the fourth floor as well."

"But what if the room can help us figure out what's causing it?" I asked. "And if the Book of Questions is up there too…"

"I know." She swore under her breath. "You know, I really do blame Aunt Candace's mask. Nothing short of a curse can cause this much havoc."

"What're we supposed to do?" I queried. "I mean, she was wearing the damn thing the last time I saw her. We can hardly grab it off her and take it to the curse breaker."

Estelle went quiet. "I'll figure something out to distract her. I'll wait until dinnertime. She won't be wearing the mask then."

To top everything off, I did not get a date with Xavier that night. He messaged me saying his boss had him running some errand again and that he'd tell me more when we next saw one another. I translated that as "when my boss lets me out," which brought a new wave of resentment towards the grumpy Reaper. It wasn't Xavier's fault, though, so I gritted my teeth and replied that I'd speak to him tomorrow. That would have to do.

That evening, we sat down to dinner—burned—and when Aunt Candace entered the room, the ceiling fell in. A hasty flick from Aunt Adelaide's wand stopped the torrent of plaster from falling on our heads, but a flurry of dust enveloped the entire room. Only Aunt Candace escaped, springing backwards like a cat.

"I'm going to order takeout from my research cave," she announced over her shoulder. "Let me know when the coast is clear."

Coughing, I lifted my gaze to see a bookshelf had fallen through the ceiling, and only Aunt Adelaide's quick actions had stopped the shelf and its contents from landing on our heads. After grabbing my own wand, I cast a levitation spell to help Aunt Adelaide steady the collapsing ceiling, and Estelle cast one on the bookshelf to push it back into the room above.

"We'll use a repair spell." Aunt Adelaide reached for her Biblio-Witch Inventory. "Ready?"

"Sure." I pulled out my own book and ran my fingertip down the page for the right word.

Estelle counted down from three, and all of us tapped on the word *repair* at the same moment.

In a flash, the ceiling knitted itself back together. The sound of the bookshelf above falling over again brought a fresh cloud of dust billowing downward, but the ceiling held, and I breathed out.

"This has gone too far." Aunt Adelaide spoke for all three of us. "I'm going to call the curse breaker."

"And I'll call the fish-and-chip shop and order us dinner," said Estelle, eyeing our dust-covered plates ruefully.

"I'll make sure nothing else is falling apart up there," I offered, since my bedroom was on the same floor as the part that had collapsed.

I trod gingerly up the stairs, concerned they might collapse, too, but I made it to the first floor in one piece.

Then I walked into my bedroom to find someone hovering directly above my bed—a male figure, transparent and wispy around the edges like an out-of-focus photograph.

"Who—?" I'd been about to ask, *Who are you*, but I knew who he was. And even if I'd never seen a ghost before—let alone *his* ghost—the man's transparency made it clear that this guy was not part of the land of the living.

"Can you help me?" Calvin Honeywood asked. "I think I've been murdered."

9

The ghost could only be one person. Calvin wasn't wearing the costume he'd worn on the night of his death, just a plain T-shirt and jeans, but I recognised his face without a doubt, and besides, no other ghost would have shown up in the library.

Why is he in my room, though?

The floor beneath my bed gave an ominous creak. "Are you the one who's been knocking things over in the library?"

The ghost didn't reply, but when another creak came from below my bookshelf, I backed towards the door. "I'll be back in a minute."

I ran out of my room and back downstairs to the kitchen, where Estelle was cleaning up the debris caused by the collapsing ceiling.

"There's a ghost in my room," I told her. "I think it's Calvin Honeywood."

Her mouth dropped open. "Oh. *He's* the one who's been knocking everything askew?"

"Looks that way." It also looked as if we owed an apology

to Aunt Candace, because even if her mask *was* cursed, it couldn't possibly have conjured up a ghost. "I'll tell Aunt Adelaide she doesn't need to call the curse breaker."

"No, I will," Estelle said. "You should get that ghost out of your room before he wrecks the place. He must be a pretty strong poltergeist to affect the library on that level."

"Why'd he show up here?" I asked. "I mean, don't ghosts usually appear in the place where they died?"

"Sometimes, but they often appear in places where they spent a lot of time while they were alive," she said. "He might have come in from outside too. He died on Samhain, when the veil between realms was thinner than usual, which gives spirits more leeway."

"I also *saw* Xavier send him into the afterworld." How had he managed to come back?

"Ghosts have more power than usual at this time of year," she said. "That must be why. I'm not an expert, though."

Xavier is. Not that I could ask him until tomorrow. "I hope his family doesn't find out. We don't need Cecilia coming here and questioning him about the inheritance."

"Oh no." Her face fell. "I bet that's why he came back. Unfinished business is the usual reason spirits stick around after death."

"What? To solve his own murder?" That did sound plausible, but I could only imagine the chaos that would ensue if we added a ghost to the army of Honeywoods swarming the police station—if he could even leave the library, which was debatable. Ghosts were usually tied to one place and were unable to leave. "I guess that's why the guardian kicked me out of the fourth-floor corridor too. It doesn't want a ghost getting in."

"Exactly," said Estelle. "That makes it all the more important that we get rid of him as fast as possible. Can you bring him downstairs?"

"Sure."

I climbed the stairs back to my room and found Calvin morosely trying to turn on the light switch without any success.

"My family can help you," I told him. "Come with me."

He turned around, and my bookshelf slid forward several inches. I tensed. "Are you doing that?"

"Sorry!" He winced. "Things move around whenever I try to touch anything."

"Well… maybe try not to." What was he? A poltergeist? We'd had ghosts in the library before but nothing like this.

Calvin drifted out of my room and followed me downstairs, where Estelle stepped in to distract him while I tracked down Aunt Adelaide. As it turned out, my aunt hadn't been able to get through to the curse breaker on the phone, which at least meant we wouldn't be on Mr Bennet's bad side for wasting his time.

Aunt Adelaide and Estelle took charge of the ghost, who seemed surprisingly cooperative with their explicit instructions to stay out of certain rooms. I didn't entirely trust him, given the amount of havoc he'd caused all day—or longer, if it'd been him bothering the library from the start. The timing of the chaos in the library suggested he'd shown up within a day of his death at most, but he hadn't shown his face at first. Yet when my family members asked, he responded with blank-faced confusion. It became apparent that Calvin didn't remember a thing about his death—that hadn't changed—but if his own unsolved murder was what had brought him back to the library, we'd have to get to the bottom of the matter if we wanted him to move on.

Oh, and we needed to send his family packing, too, preferably without them finding out he was here. The thought of them running rampant around the library was

even less appealing than watching Aunt Candace do an inter-
pretive dance while wearing that creepy mask.

I hope Calvin can identify his killer, I thought. *If he can't,
who can?*

———

I wasn't sure what was worse—being woken by a ghost or
being woken by Sylvester—but this time I was jolted out of
sleep to the alarming sight of the ghost hovering above my
head, upside down.

"I was bored," was his explanation. "Everyone else was
asleep."

"So was I." I squinted suspiciously at him. "You haven't
moved anything else around in the night, have you?"

"No."

Hmm. Did I trust him? After the rest of his family's
behaviour, his meek demeanour was welcome enough, but it
might be an act. Maybe his jittery nature was a consequence
of growing up in a family like that, but the level of destruction he'd caused made me suspect he was more than he
seemed.

The only silver lining to having a ghost in my room was
that I now had a solid excuse to speak to Xavier. Whatever
the Grim Reaper had to say, this was far more important
than his grudge against me for betraying his trust, so I
ordered the ghost to wait downstairs so I could get dressed
in peace. Then I sent a message to Xavier—or tried to. As
usual, my phone connection refused to cooperate, and I gave
up on the fifth attempt and went downstairs.

When I reached the kitchen, I found that the ghost had
successfully dragged Estelle out of her room too. She sat
sleepily at the table with the ghost hovering at her side,

looking mournfully at her bowl of cornflakes. Sylvester, notably, was absent from his usual spot. Probably, he didn't want to get involved with our transparent new visitor.

"Hey, Rory," Estelle said sleepily.

"I can't get hold of Xavier," I said delicately, not wanting to refer to him as the Reaper and freak out the ghost. "I'm going to have to walk to his house."

She raised a brow. "Are you sure you-know-who will like that?"

"Nope, but I have a legitimate reason."

I'd *seen* Xavier send Calvin's spirit to the afterlife. The image wouldn't leave my mind that easily. Calvin himself supposedly didn't remember a thing, but if he was lying, a Reaper would have a better chance of unearthing the truth than the rest of us would.

I left the library and walked across the square towards the high street. It was another cold, drizzly day, the rain soaking into my hood, and as I crossed the square, I began to have second thoughts—not just about going outside. Potentially antagonising the Grim Reaper again when there was no telling whether Xavier would actually be able to help was a risky move. Still, I wouldn't know unless I tried.

Shivering, I opened the cemetery gate, passing rows of graves as I walked up the path to the large house in which the two Reapers lived. When I reached the door, I knocked. Then I held my breath and waited.

The door swung inward, soundless, and the Grim Reaper waited on the other side, his scythe held aloft. Into the silence, he intoned, "No, you may not see my apprentice."

"I thought you and he had come to an understanding." Frustration rose inside me, despite the looming presence of the scythe above my head. "I thought I was allowed to visit his house, at the very least."

"Don't test me, Aurora. You and Xavier schemed and broke the Reapers' rules behind my back. You're lucky I'm willing to allow you any contact at all."

"You're not in charge of his life." I gave up on that line of argument for now. "That's not why I came anyway. We have a ghost in the library."

"What ghost?" Xavier appeared behind his boss. "Not—?"

"Calvin Honeywood," I confirmed. "He showed up in my room."

Xavier stared at me over his boss's shadowy shoulder. "I banished him. You saw that, didn't you?"

"Yes, and he came back," I said. "No idea why."

"Does he remember anything?"

I shook my head. "That's why I came here. The others said maybe Calvin returned because he had unfinished business. Like solving his murder. That and he died on Samhain, which can have weird aftereffects, can't it?"

"Yes," Xavier said. "I'll come—"

"I will get rid of him myself," said the Grim Reaper. "My apprentice will not."

I frowned. "I'm not asking you to get rid of him. The police are still investigating his murder, remember? He might be able to help them find his killer."

"That's my offer. Take it or leave it."

"You're being incredibly petty." I knew that comment wouldn't get me anything other than a door slammed in my face, but my frustration peaked when Xavier tried to approach me but found his way blocked by a wall of Reaper.

The door swung closed. I stepped back off the doorstep, raindrops dripping down my face, and was halfway to knocking again before I thought better of it. *So much for that idea.*

Resigned, I walked back to the library. I hadn't handled that in the best way, I'd freely admit, but going to the

Reapers' house had been an impulse decision in the first place. I'd known the Grim Reaper would have zero curiosity as to why Calvin had come back from the afterworld. If he couldn't swing his scythe at the problem, he simply wasn't interested.

Estelle looked up hopefully when I came into the library, but I just shrugged, not wanting to mention the word *Reaper* with Calvin in hearing distance. From what I'd gathered, most spirits were terrified of all Reapers, and that he'd gone willingly into the afterworld a few days ago didn't mean he necessarily wanted a repeat performance.

While Aunt Adelaide moved in to talk to the ghost, Estelle walked over to me and whispered, "No luck?"

"The boss said he'd come and deal with the problem." I didn't need to give any more detail than that. "He had no interest in finding the killer or in anything else."

"Harsh," she said. "I think we've exhausted all routes of questioning here, to tell you the truth. He doesn't remember anything else."

"Did you tell him Edwin's investigating his death?"

"Yes, but…"

"Not about his family being here?" I guessed. Once they found out Calvin was at the library, they'd certainly want to talk to him, and an influx of Cecilia Honeywood and her other relatives was not what the library needed.

"No," Estelle answered. "He seems shaken up enough already. Xavier wasn't able to get away?"

"Nope, his boss is being completely irrational." I dropped my gaze. "I know that letting the ghost stick around here isn't exactly within the rules, but he refused to consider anything other than… banishment." I lowered my voice on the last word in case the ghost was listening to us talking.

"What if he shows up anyway?"

The thought had crossed my mind. "I doubt he wants to

risk his apprentice slipping from his clutches. I told him he was being irrational, which has likely lowered me even further in his estimation."

Estelle winced. "Might be time to be honest with the ghost."

I ducked back into the living quarters and approached the spirit, but the question that came out of my mouth was "Did you know your entire family was in town?"

"No. Oh *no*." Calvin threw his hands over his face, and a nearby bookshelf began to fall in slow motion. While Aunt Adelaide hastily moved to steady it, the ghost drifted forward, wringing his hands. "Say it isn't true."

"Afraid so," I said. "They want to know about the inheritance, since you didn't leave a will."

"Of course I didn't." He looked at me as if I had three heads. "How was I supposed to know I'd drop dead in a week?"

"After inheriting from your dad, right?" Estelle jumped on the subject. "Do you think any of them might've been involved in your death? Your family members, I mean?"

"No... I don't *think* so." His voice crackled like a dying phone signal, as if to reflect his agitation. "I don't know *how*, either. I haven't seen them since the funeral."

"When was that?" I asked.

"Last week," he replied. "If one of them made me like this, it's their own fault they can't get the inheritance, isn't it?"

He had a point. "Erm, what about that business partner of yours?"

"Dwight!" he said. "What's *he* up to? He was at the party, too, I remember."

"You do remember the party?" Estelle pressed. "I thought you didn't remember that night at all."

"It's a blur, but I remember being in the library," he said.

"It's the last place I recall, in fact. Maybe that's why I came back here."

"We were wondering that," I said. "Any ideas?"

"Maybe because this is where it… happened," he said. "I bet Dwight put a curse on me while I wasn't paying attention."

"You think it was a curse that killed you?" I asked. "Why would Dwight do that? You used to be friends, right?"

"We had a falling-out," he mumbled. "Business disagreement. He wasn't happy when I got the money either."

Hmm. He hadn't seen his attacker, so there was certainly a possibility that Dwight had been responsible, but that also didn't mean that Calvin's own family hadn't been involved either. Certainly, some curses took several days or weeks to take effect. How could he be sure it'd happened in the library?

"Also, someone stole your prize," I added. "Someone dressed as a fairy. Do you remember anything about that?"

"No." He frowned. "What prize? Oh… the raffle. Yes… I remember winning, but I don't remember what I did with the prize. What was it? A toy pumpkin?"

Estelle nodded. "Someone who was there said the person who stole it was wearing a fairy costume. Ring any bells?"

His expression cleared. "Bernadette Miller. I saw her staring at it all night. I bet she waited until I was drunk and then stole my prize when I wasn't paying attention."

"Are you sure?" We didn't need any more false alarms. Of course, stealing a toy pumpkin didn't mean the thief had been involved in his murder.

"Positive," he said. "She tried to swipe it from me while I was at the buffet too."

Estelle frowned. "I thought you didn't remember anything about the party."

"More details are coming back the longer I spend here,"

said the ghost. "You aren't going to tell my family I'm here, are you?"

"We'll speak to Edwin first," I decided. "Estelle?"

"You go. I'll stay here."

I figured that she and Aunt Adelaide had a better chance of stopping the ghost from destroying the place than I did, but there was one slight issue. "What if Edwin wants to come here?"

"I don't think Edwin or the trolls can even *see* ghosts," Aunt Adelaide remarked.

"That's a good point." Most people couldn't. Even among witches and wizards, only about a third had that ability, though it'd also be just our luck if everyone in the Honeywood family could see him as well. "I won't mention him unless I have to, then."

"Please don't tell anyone," Calvin said morosely. "I don't need to be made a spectacle of."

"I won't," I promised.

Not unless I have to, I added silently.

I walked out into the rain again, huddled inside my cloak. Part of me hoped Xavier might have escaped his boss, though it seemed unlikely after my impromptu visit had riled up the Grim Reaper even further. Knowing my luck, I figured the Grim Reaper had concluded that I'd somehow brought the ghost back myself, but letting the Grim Reaper banish Calvin would do nothing either to solve the murder or to win forgiveness from our resident scythe-wielding grump.

Pity he can't banish the other Honeywoods instead, I thought, crossing my fingers that they'd given Edwin a break.

No luck. When I reached the seafront, the strident sound of Cecilia's voice greeted me at the doors to the police station.

A tired-looking Edwin sat at his desk within a sea of

Honeywoods, and he looked up hopefully when I came in. "Yes?"

"Can I talk to you alone, Edwin?"

"No." I heard that less as a refusal and more as an admission that it would be impossible to get him alone at any time soon. "Is it urgent?"

"No…" I caught the eye of one of the trolls at the back of the room and tried to signal that I'd appreciate them getting Cecilia out of our hair for a bit. "No, but I have information that might be relevant."

"What information?" Cecilia swooped in, eyeing me suspiciously. "You know who killed Calvin?"

"No." I had to make that clear.

"Then why would you waste the police's time?"

Is she joking? If I'd been someone else—maybe Cass—I'd have pointed out her hypocrisy, but I didn't quite have the nerve to.

Luckily, the troll responded to my silent pleas and stepped forward. "We can keep an eye on things here for a minute while you talk to Edwin."

The elf policeman rose to his feet. "Fine."

His tone implied "This had better be worth it." I wasn't sure it would be, but it'd be a balm to Edwin's sanity to have a little time away from the scourge of Honeywoods. I followed him into a side room, and he closed the door on Cecilia's objections.

"Can't you get your trolls to shake some sense into her?" I asked him in an undertone. "I mean, she's the one wasting police time."

"She's been calling the office all night," he muttered. "Claimed she had a list of suspects. She'd been asking everyone at all the pubs last night for a list of people who attended the party. What did you want anyway?"

"I got the name of the person who might have stolen

Calvin's prize," I explained. "Bernadette Miller. Do you know her?"

"Yes." He paused. "She was on the list."

"Of people who attended the party? Isn't that the whole town?"

His eyes narrowed. "More or less."

Oops. He probably hadn't appreciated the reminder that he hadn't been able to attend the party himself. "Do you know where she lives, or…?"

"Are you done in there?" Cecilia asked loudly from the other side of the door.

I winced. "I know stealing the prize isn't proof of someone being guilty of murder, but it's the first new name we've had, and—"

Edwin ground his teeth. "I don't have time to go searching for … What was it? A toy ghost?"

"Pumpkin."

He exhaled a sigh. "Sorry, Rory, but I can't afford to leave the station unless we're following a genuine lead."

And even then, he'd be pursued by an unwanted group of Honeywoods intent on enacting justice. If Bernadette did have the toy pumpkin, getting it back wouldn't do anything to help Calvin—unless she'd seen his killer.

"If she did steal the prize, she stole from the library. Technically." That was Sylvester-style logic, I knew, but if Bernadette *had* seen the killer and Edwin's hands were tied, who else would deliver her into his hands? "Estelle is the one who ran the raffle in the first place."

Theoretically, if ghosts counted as people, the pumpkin was Calvin's property instead, but I didn't dare bring *that* up with Cecilia on the other side of the door. Besides, Calvin was unable to leave the library.

"Yes," he relented. "That's true. Does Estelle know this Bernadette person?"

"I don't know, but she can probably find her."

He gave a nod. "All right."

Was that permission? I opened my mouth to ask, but Cecilia nudged the door inward. "If you two have quite finished, we have a long list of suspects to get through!"

Taking that as a sign to leave, I edged out of the room and made my way through the tide of Honeywoods to the door.

Once outside, I walked back to the library swiftly.

While I'd been unsure if Estelle would agree to paying Bernadette a visit, she accepted my logic with a nod. "Yeah, we stand a better chance of being able to visit her than poor Edwin does."

"It feels underhanded," I admitted. "Yes, the pumpkin is the library's property… or Calvin's, at any rate, but we aren't the police."

"No, but I've visited Bernadette several times before when she's 'forgotten' to return a book," she remarked. "I looked her up. She's on our list of persistent nuisances who've stacked up late fees, and I'm pretty sure she's tried to take books home without checking them out at least once too. She seems like exactly the sort who'd steal a toy pumpkin from someone who was drunk."

"I told you so," Calvin put in. "She stole my prize."

"You want to visit her?" Aunt Adelaide guessed. "I can watch the desk."

"Edwin didn't say we couldn't pay her a house visit," I added to Estelle. "I think he'd have given us direct permission if Cecilia hadn't barged in."

"All right." Estelle set her shoulders. "I wonder if I'll find any more of our books in her house too."

"Seems a good enough excuse to check on her," I agreed as we turned to leave. "I know it's not much of a lead on the murder, though."

"She might have seen the killer," Estelle said. "Not that we can trust anything she says. I seem to remember that she came up with all kinds of elaborate excuses as to why she was six months late returning a book."

"Should we tell her about the ghost?" I asked as we left the library. "I didn't even get the chance to tell Edwin. Cecilia was hovering outside the door the whole time, and I didn't dare risk it."

"I'm surprised the trolls haven't locked her up," she said. "Granted, she'd probably talk her way out of her cell by threatening to bring the roof down on their heads. Coven leaders have a flair for the dramatic."

"Especially her."

Bernadette turned out to live in a small cul-de-sac off the road that ran parallel to the seafront. Estelle rapped on the door to a small cottage, and a petite witch answered.

Bernadette blinked her large, innocent eyes at Estelle. "I didn't forget another book, did I?"

"Not exactly," Estelle said. "I'm told you may have taken something belonging to Calvin Honeywood when you were at our Halloween party."

"No," Bernadette Miller said at once. "I didn't. Whoever told you that was lying."

Her tone was overly defensive for someone supposedly innocent. I glanced over her shoulder, and my gaze snagged on something large and distinctly pumpkin-shaped in the background. "What's that over there?"

"Nothing." She stepped into the way to block my vision— too late.

"I don't think so," Estelle said. "You know that Calvin is dead, don't you? That pumpkin is now the library's property, and we'd like it back."

A flush spread over her face. "It's mine. I bought it from the shop."

"Can you show us the receipt?"

"I don't have to talk to you." She made to close the door.

On impulse, I said, "Calvin's ghost told us you stole from him."

She went completely still, and the colour drained from her face. "What?"

"His ghost showed up in the library today," Estelle said. "He'd like his prize back."

Bernadette stared at us as though I'd produced Xavier's scythe from behind my back. Then her shoulders slumped. "He... All right."

She left the door swinging on its hinges, ran back inside, and returned with the pumpkin toy, which she all but threw at us.

Estelle caught it in one hand. "Before we go, I wanted to ask if you saw anyone else paying attention to him at the party. Anyone who might have been involved in what happened to him later that night?"

"No," she said. "I'm not the one who—killed him."

"Aren't you?" Edwin came running up the path behind us, breathless. "I think you should come and answer some questions, Bernadette."

"I'm innocent!" She shrank away from him, into the doorway of her house. "Just ask Calvin's ghost."

At the word *ghost*, Edwin raised a brow, but he beckoned to her. "If you're innocent, this won't take long. Come on."

"I... All right." She trailed out of the house with her head down and followed him down the street.

Luckily, the police station wasn't far—which was probably why Edwin had managed to get here in the first place— and Bernadette didn't attempt to escape en route. While Edwin handed her over to the trolls for questioning, Cecilia bombarded him with a torrent of questions of her own. Estelle stepped in and told the Honeywoods the gist of the situation without mentioning our ghostly visitor. Kind of impressive, really.

Edwin, however, was not to be easily fooled. While Cecilia's attention was on Estelle, he approached me and muttered, "Now, Rory, what's all this about a ghost?"

10

I glanced at Cecilia then addressed Edwin in a whisper. "At the library. He, ah, told us not to tell anyone he was there."

Edwin's eyes bulged. "He came back?"

"Who's back?" Cecilia demanded.

"Dwight Keaton," Estelle blurted, presumably improvising. "Did you finish questioning him?"

"Yes," Edwin said. "I sent him home. Any reason?"

Yes. The ghost accused him of murder. Aloud, I said, "It might be worth talking to him again."

"Dwight Keaton?" Cecilia asked sharply. "Calvin's slimy ex-business partner? Yes, we should question him immediately."

"No, we shall not," Edwin said. *"I'll* question him, and if he turns out to be guilty, I'll take action myself."

Cecilia took a step back, wearing an affronted expression. "I am the leader of the Honeywood Coven!"

"And I'm head of the police force in Ivory Beach, which isn't part of your coven's domain," he retorted. "Now, I'll kindly ask you to go home while I go and pay Dwight a visit."

113

I blinked in surprise at his firm tone. I hadn't thought Edwin had it in him, but the Honeywoods must have finally pushed him over the edge.

Cecilia turned the colour of beetroot, which clashed dramatically with her hair. "How dare you!"

Estelle nudged me towards the door and then stepped in to talk to Cecilia. "There's plenty for you to do while Edwin's busy talking to Dwight."

Edwin himself made a swift getaway, joining me at the door with his face as flushed as Cecilia's.

"I am *at my limit* with her," he said as the door slid closed behind us. "Are all coven leaders that domineering?"

"I've not met enough to know," I said. "Anyway, you *do* have authority here. She doesn't."

"We're a small police force," he said. "Her coven could make our lives very uncomfortable if they put their minds to it, and your cousin won't be able to distract her forever. Now, *why* exactly is Calvin's ghost in your library?"

I gave Edwin a summary of the library's ghostly infestation as we walked across the seafront. Edwin took it better than I'd expected, though in fairness, the poor guy had been dealing with enough nightmarish *living* people for the past few days that a ghost was nothing in comparison.

"I figured you wouldn't want Cecilia Honeywood to know," I added. "Calvin certainly doesn't want to talk to them."

"You mean *you* don't want her showing up at the library," he said. "As a coven leader, she's very likely to be able to see ghosts herself."

"What would that achieve?" I asked. "He doesn't remember his death, and he told us he didn't write a will either. The guy can't touch anything without knocking half the library's shelves over. We don't need him getting worked up for no good reason."

"Nevertheless," he said. "Did he really accuse Dwight Keaton of killing him, or was that just a ploy to distract Cecilia?"

"Yes, he did," I said. "He was pretty clear on it."

"Dwight's house is this way." He pointed northward. "I wouldn't normally bring you to speak to a suspect…"

"But I think you might need someone to watch your back in case Cecilia follows us," I finished.

Edwin sighed, but he didn't disagree. "Frankly, I hope this Dwight *is* our culprit. It'll make all our lives easier if we put the matter to rest."

True, and getting rid of Calvin Honeywood's family was an understandable priority for Edwin… but Dwight's guilt also seemed too good to be true. For one, Dwight had still been at the party at the time of Calvin's death, unless he'd intentionally returned to the library after committing the deed to take attention off himself. Then there was the question of *how* he'd killed Calvin. He might not have needed to be present in person, especially if he'd had an accomplice. But who might that have been?

Dwight's house stood on the other side of the town square, and walking there alone with Edwin was decidedly awkward. My attempts to talk were met with grunts, so I gave up and walked in silence until we reached a narrow street where a house three storeys taller than its neighbours caught my eye. Its roof had been sculpted to be shaped like a wizard's hat and painted a bright shade of orange. *Is that the place?*

Edwin approached the house without comment; after a moment of confusion, I remembered that Dwight and Calvin had both worked in magical construction. Evidently, they'd practised on their own houses too.

When Edwin knocked on the peculiarly oval-shaped door, Dwight answered. He looked slightly less dishevelled than when Edwin had hauled him out of the party in a half-drunk state but not much.

"Edwin," he said. "Didn't I already answer all your questions?"

"New developments have come to light," Edwin said. "Namely, an accusation directly from the victim's ghost himself."

"Calvin… is a ghost?" he asked blankly.

"That's right."

I hadn't expected Edwin to mention Calvin's return from the death right away, but it certainly got a reaction. Just like Bernadette had, Dwight went pale, and he pressed a hand against the wall to steady himself. "He's… Calvin is really back?"

"Yes," I said. "He showed up in the library, and he refuses to leave until his killer is brought to justice."

"I'm not the killer!" Dwight insisted. "Calvin doesn't remember anything about his death, does he? He's assuming I killed him because of our argument."

"What would make you assume he doesn't remember?" Edwin narrowed his eyes. "I think you should come back with me to answer some more questions."

Dwight flinched. "Is the ghost at the police station?"

"No, Rory already told you he's at the library." Edwin beckoned to him. "Come on."

Dwight's mouth turned down at the corners. "I didn't lay a finger on him."

Nevertheless, he followed Edwin out of the house without raising a fuss. Walking back to the police station was even more awkward than our journey to Dwight's house, but my impulse to return to the library was tempered by the knowledge that Estelle would probably appreciate being rescued from Cecilia. She'd done us a huge favour keeping her from following us to Dwight's house.

When we reached the seafront, Edwin entered the police station first, and Cecilia and the other Honeywoods descended on him like a swarm of seagulls. Estelle seized the chance to escape with me, and we hurried outside.

"I was hoping you wouldn't take long," she whispered. "I had to talk Cecilia out of going to the library to look for clues. We don't need her to notice we have a new resident."

"Definitely not." When we were at a safe distance from the station, I told her about Dwight's odd reaction to the news of Calvin's return. "He spoke pretty confidently when he said Calvin can't possibly know who killed him, which seems suspicious. Maybe Edwin's right."

"You think Dwight's guilty?" Estelle asked.

"I know it seems too obvious," I said. "It would solve all our problems if he was. Cecilia thinks he's guilty, too, so he might be safer behind bars."

Estelle snorted. "You aren't wrong, but when he said that Calvin wouldn't remember who killed him, he might have meant that ghosts don't usually remember their deaths. It's not that unique."

"That's common knowledge?" Sometimes I still tripped over which pieces of information on the magical world were widely known and which were confined to my unique situation. Dating a Reaper gave me more access to knowledge of all things ghostly than the average person.

"Common enough," she said. "One in three witches and wizards can see them. Also, he didn't know Calvin would come back from the dead, did he?"

"I guess not." He'd been surprised, but some of his reaction had been decidedly off. Did that point to guilt? *Well, that's up to Edwin to decide.*

We walked into the library. Aunt Adelaide remained by the desk, but the murmur of voices from the living quarters pointed to the ghost's location.

Inside the living room, Aunt Candace sat on the sofa, while the ghost chattered away with an enthusiasm that reminded me of my familiar. Her pen and notebook floated beside her, ink flying everywhere as her enchanted pen tried to keep up with Calvin's speech.

"Aurora, I demand an apology!" Aunt Candace jumped to her feet. "My mask had nothing to do with the incidents in the library. This ghost did."

Calvin flinched, knocking a stack of books off the coffee table. "I didn't do it on purpose!"

"Of course you didn't." Aunt Candace glared at us. "Well?"

"Sorry, Aunt Candace," I said.

To Calvin, I added, "The police are questioning Dwight again."

"Good." He looked back at Aunt Candace. "Er, your pen didn't write that down, did it?"

"What are you even talking about?" Estelle asked.

"Magical architecture," Aunt Candace replied. "It's vital work for my next novel. Go away."

"We thought Calvin would want to know the developments in the police's investigation into his murder," I pointed out. "Also, his family almost came to the library to look for clues. You had a narrow escape."

"What?" Calvin yelped, and the sofa slid forward into the back of Aunt Candace's legs, nearly causing her to trip over.

She caught her balance and glared at me again. "Stop upsetting him."

"He wants to know who's responsible for his death, doesn't he?" I pointed out. "Luckily, Estelle talked Cecilia out of coming here. I hope she won't stop Edwin from getting a confession from Dwight."

"He'll confess," said Calvin.

He sounded almost *too* sure of himself. I tilted my head,

trying to read his expression. "What of the inheritance? That's the real reason Cecilia and the others are here."

His face crumpled. "I can't… I can't even *spend* it now."

He turned away, and as he did so, the nearby bookshelf began to topple forward. Aunt Candace reacted with surprising swiftness, whipping her wand out before it hit the floor, but the ghost had already floated through the wall and vanished.

Aunt Candace tutted. "Now look what you've done."

"You haven't met his family yet, have you?" I asked, though I felt a twinge of guilt. "They're driving Edwin into an early grave by pestering him about that inheritance."

"She's right," Estelle added. "Anyway—isn't the whole reason Calvin stuck around because he had unfinished business?"

While she talked to Aunt Candace, I went looking for the ghost in the lobby and spied Sylvester perched amongst the reference books behind the desk.

"Did *you* know there was a ghost in here before we did?" I asked him.

"I know everything" was his helpful reply.

"And you thought it was funny not to tell us." He'd let us assume Aunt Candace's mask was behind the chaos, probably for his own amusement. "What of the Book of Questions, then? Why would the library hide it from a ghost? It's not like he can use it."

"What did I tell you about asking me questions?"

"I can't ask the book, can I?" I knew he'd take even *that* as a question, but I couldn't resist. "Is the guardian afraid of ghosts now?"

The owl gave a loud hoot and turned his back on me, which I really should have expected from my mention of the guardian. Sylvester and the library's other sentient magical entity were not friends.

I should have known better than to ask.

The day didn't improve much as time went on. More minor disasters occurred, but it was impossible to tell whether the ghost was responsible or it was just plain bad luck. Doors were found closed, shelves moved, and some alarming sneezing noises issued from the third floor that I could only assume came from the manticore. The others and I universally agreed to leave Cass to deal with that one.

Only Aunt Candace was in a comparatively good mood, despite her annoyance at us for driving off the ghost. She'd taken up residence in the lobby's corner, her notebook and pen bobbing up and down as she presumably penned something based on the ghost's stories.

My own spirits remained low—no thanks to the *actual* spirit hiding somewhere among the shelves—and even a knock on the front door didn't improve my mood until I found Xavier on the other side. *Oh right.* He was ever the gentleman, not wanting to invite himself into the library without permission. His boss could stand to learn some manners, really.

"You're here." I wrapped my arms tightly around Xavier, some of the tension seeping out of me. "How'd you give your boss the slip?"

"I convinced him to let me outside," he replied, hugging me back. "Where's this ghost?"

I released him. "I don't know. He's still touchy about being dead, and whenever he so much as goes near a bookshelf, it falls over."

"He's in the Reading Corner," Estelle said from behind the front desk. "I saw him a minute ago."

"All right." I beckoned to Xavier. "Better tread carefully."

"He's a ghost, not a grenade," said Aunt Candace as we walked past her seat. "You'd better not banish him, Reaper. He and I need to have another interview."

"Ignore her," I told him. "She's been questioning him about magical construction, I think."

"Ah." Xavier wore a dubious expression as he followed me towards the back of the library. None of our visitors had stayed long, so the Reading Corner was a quiet open space. The ghost perched on the edge of the hammock, more floating than sitting, a pensive look on his face.

At least until he saw Xavier's scythe. Then he jumped upward with a cry of "Reaper!"

"I'm not going to hurt you," said Xavier. "I want to know what you remember about your death... or to be more precise, how you came back from the other side after I banished you. Do you remember?"

The ghost recoiled, and the hammock rocked back and forth. More alarmingly, the surrounding shelves began to shake too.

"Don't panic," I told him. "Xavier isn't here to banish you again. We want to find your killer."

"No." Calvin shook his head violently. "Leave me alone!"

Xavier took a step forward, and the ghost lurched backwards with such violence that his transparent body bent like a boomerang. I reached for my wand too late, as the shelves fell into one another in a crescendo of noise. I held my hands over my head as Xavier swept me away from the shower of books tumbling off shelves and crashing to the floor.

When the crashing finally subsided, I edged forward to check on the damage. The ghost had collapsed the entire Fiction section, but Calvin himself was nowhere to be seen.

"Rory!" Estelle approached at a run, her wand held aloft. "Are you all right?"

"Yeah. I'm fine." I lowered my hands from my head. "He got freaked out by the Reaper. Where'd he go?"

"I should leave before he does any more damage," Xavier

said apologetically. "I shouldn't have tried to talk to him at all. My boss already made it clear that I shouldn't."

"It's not your fault." My heart gave a twinge. "He'll get over it. Listen, are you free later?"

"I should be." He gave a ghost of a smile—pun intended. "At least my boss can't argue against me checking up on a local spirit. I'll use that excuse as long as Calvin stays in the library."

"Just as long as he doesn't plan on banishing Calvin himself," I said. "Ghosts aren't normally that strong, are they?"

"No, but he's a poltergeist and one who came back on Samhain," he replied. "I can search for him in the afterworld if you want me to get a closer look at him and see if there's anything off."

"That'd definitely freak him out," I said. "I don't know if I'm just being paranoid, but… well, the Book of Questions has been missing since he came back, and the guardian of the fourth-floor corridor has locked us out. I assumed it was because the library didn't want the ghost getting into either of those places. Though I suppose there's still the chance it might be Aunt Candace's cursed mask instead."

"Cursed mask?" he echoed. "Is that still around?"

"Unfortunately," I said. "I think it's the ghost, though. Why'd he come back in the first place? When one of the doors to the afterworld closes, it's supposed to be permanent, isn't it? Even on Samhain."

"Usually," he confirmed. "I'd have expected my boss to take more interest in the situation, to tell you the truth. It's not one I'm familiar with."

"He's letting his anger at both of us cloud his judgement," I surmised. "I guess I didn't help when I yelled at him."

"No, he deserved it," he said. "He *was* being ridiculous, even if he's had a lot on his mind lately."

That was true, but between our exploits with the Founders and their insinuation that the Reapers had helped in their scheming, how could I stay away when my life was so intertwined with Xavier's that even the Grim Reaper hadn't been able to deny it?

"Yeah." I contemplated the mess in the Reading Corner. "I guess that's my afternoon sorted, but I'll see you later?"

"Sure." He gave me another hug. "I'll message you."

I hope the boss lets you. Granted, going to the Black Dog pub ran the risk of us ending up surrounded by Honeywoods, but if he came to the library instead, having dinner in the company of a ghost wasn't my idea of a fun night either, especially when the mere sight of a Reaper had caused Calvin to destroy half the first floor.

No, the only way to be rid of the ghost, short of wielding a scythe, was to solve his murder—which meant finding out what secrets Calvin Honeywood was hiding.

11

The ghost remained absent long after Xavier had left the library. It took Estelle and me close to an hour to restore the Reading Corner to its former state, and we found no signs of the destructive ghost on the ground floor. Eventually, we tracked Calvin down by the sound of books falling off the shelves on the first floor as he drifted among the stacks.

"Can you not do that?" Estelle asked him. "You're scaring off our visitors."

The ghost looked affronted. "I'm not doing it on purpose."

Right. As I watched him float away through a nearby wall, I thought she'd been lenient with him. Really, in his own way, the guy was almost as much of a menace as the rest of his family, but we needed his cooperation if we wanted a chance of solving his murder.

Mentioning the inheritance was a sore point, I knew, but it was also the reason his family was in town in the first place. Xavier said it wasn't that unusual for ghosts to be a little touchy, but if he refused to acknowledge the issue that had got him murdered, how were we supposed to help him move on to the next world?

"I wish I could ask the Book of Questions," I said to Estelle. "Something's bugging me about that guy, but Xavier said he looked like a normal ghost, despite being a poltergeist."

"Yeah, he'd know if something was off with him," Estelle said. "Though I doubt most Reapers will have had experience with banishing a ghost from somewhere as unpredictable as the library."

"Maybe that's it," I agreed. "I just wish he'd cooperate a little better. I don't know how he expects us to figure out who killed him if he won't discuss his death, the inheritance, or his family members."

All we'd managed to get out of him was that he'd been estranged from his siblings and parents from the moment he'd turned eighteen and had been able to move away from his coven. That might account for how surprised Cecilia and the others had been when his father had given him the entire inheritance, though I'd gathered that most covens were usually well-off.

"Cecilia might genuinely think she needs the money," said Estelle, as though she'd picked up on my line of thinking. "I know the Honeywoods aren't a huge coven, even if they act like they are. Their town's even smaller than Ivory Beach, and we don't *have* a coven."

"Is that why they're acting so superior to Edwin?" I asked. "I know I'm not an expert in how coven hierarchies work, but that Cecilia seems to think she outranks him."

"In some towns, the coven leader does have authority over the police or at least the option to ignore their advice and take matters into their own hands," Estelle explained. "Not always, but who'd want to start a feud with that family?"

"Nobody sane." I glanced upward as a breeze lifted my hair and spied the ghost drifting upstairs. "I hope he's not going to the third floor."

"Me too," said Estelle. "The manticore has a cold. Not sure the ghost caused *that,* but anything's possible at this point."

"What about that cursed mask?"

"I think my mum forgot all about calling the curse breaker when the ghost showed up," she said. "Not sure he'll be willing to help anyway. And Aunt Candace won't let us take that mask away without a fight."

True, and the ghost was the more pressing problem at hand. Aunt Candace herself had abandoned her seat and wandered off somewhere into the living quarters, or else I might have worried that she'd overhear us.

"I hope she'll let the ghost go without a fuss, at least," I said. "She seems surprisingly friendly with him."

"That's because she's trying to steal his life story to put in a book."

"I didn't think his life was *that* interesting." I rolled my eyes. "I wonder if he shared anything else with her that might help. I know he seems to think Dwight's guilt is a given, but... I don't know."

"We can ask Aunt Candace," Estelle said dubiously. "Or... Where's your familiar?"

"Good point." I hadn't seen Jet all day, but I'd been somewhat distracted by the ghost's rampage of destruction. "I'll find him."

"I'll go after the ghost," she said. "I don't think Cass will appreciate a visit from him. If we can keep him confined to the lobby, we can at least limit the destruction."

"True." We parted ways, and I went to look for my familiar.

I searched on the shelf under the front desk in case he

was napping again and unearthed a lot of feathers but no signs of Jet.

"Looking for your crow?" Sylvester peered down at me from the top of a shelf. "He's with his favourite witch."

"Aunt Candace." I might have also pointed out that he was *my* familiar, not hers, but Sylvester knew that perfectly well already.

When I entered the living quarters, I heard clattering around in the kitchen that pointed me to Aunt Candace. As I'd suspected, Jet was perched on top of the cupboard, chattering amicably to her.

"What?" Aunt Candace asked through a mouthful of apple tart she was eating out of the fridge. "I do hope you've come to apologise."

"I already did," I reminded her. "You aren't sending Jet to spy on people again, are you?"

"Such accusations."

I swivelled to my familiar. "*Did* she send you to spy on anyone?"

"Yes, partner!" he said. "She asked me to fly to the police station and listen in on Dwight Keaton's trial!"

"Honestly!" Aunt Candace said. "You people have no concept of confidentiality."

"Maybe you ought to get your own familiar instead of stealing mine," I retaliated. "I'm pretty sure Edwin will notice a crow spying on him. I'm not sure there's even going to be a trial, besides. It depends on whether he thinks Dwight is guilty or not." *And if Cecilia gives him a moment's peace to do the questioning.*

"Oh, it's a done deal," said Aunt Candace in an offhand manner.

"What makes you say that?" I asked. "Are you taking the ghost's word for it?"

"Calvin is very misunderstood," she said. "I empathise with him."

I suppressed a snort. "Have you forgotten he's been trashing the place since he came back? Also, when you were questioning him, did he mention whether he had any plans for his will? Because that's the only thing that's going to get rid of his family before they find out he's here."

"You're lecturing the wrong person," she informed me. "I'm nothing more than an innocent bystander."

"With a habit of spying on confidential meetings." Not that Calvin's family was any better. "For whatever reason, he's willing to talk to you. Can't you persuade the ghost to vacate the library before he brings the place crashing down on our heads?"

"Bargaining now, are you?" she asked. "Very well. If I speak to the ghost, you'll have to agree to leave my mask alone. Yes, I know you were planning to take it to that awful curse breaker behind my back."

Oops. I looked pointedly at Jet, who hid his face behind a wing.

"Only because we thought your mask was causing everything to fall apart in here," I said. "You have to admit it's more plausible than a ghost coming back from the other side of the door to the afterworld."

"Oh yes." Her expression changed, becoming more animated. "It's so intriguing, isn't it? I had to ask, but when I pressed him for the details, he recalled following a bright light when he passed to the other side. Otherwise, all he remembers is waking up here in the library."

"Does he?" I asked. "I thought he forgot everything, including how he died."

"You've treated him abominably," she reprimanded me. "No wonder he'd rather talk to me instead."

"He did scare off all our visitors," I reminded her. "Let me speak to Estelle, and I'll get back to you."

I'd certainly have to check with the others to ask if they were okay with abandoning the mask in exchange for Aunt Candace's cooperation. To get rid of the ghost, it'd be worth the trade-off, though, especially if the mask wasn't involved in the current incidents at all.

"I'll tell her, partner!" Jet squeaked, perhaps feeling guilty for telling tales on us to Aunt Candace.

"I think she's upstairs, following the ghost," I said. "I hope Calvin isn't on the third floor. Cass is already in a bad mood, given that her manticore has caught a cold."

"Has he, now?" Aunt Candace cackled. "I bet it's because she let him out for a walk on Halloween."

"She didn't, did she?" I'd thought she'd stayed upstairs all night.

"Oh yes," said Aunt Candace. "I believe she used the library's magic to make her a secret staircase that led out the back door so that the manticore wouldn't stumble upon any of the guests."

I gaped at her. "She… did what?"

"What I said."

"You helped her." I couldn't even imagine what chaos might have been unleashed if the beast had escaped Cass's control. What had they both been thinking?

Jet returned before I'd quite taken in her words. "She said yes, partner!"

"Good." Aunt Candace shot me a grin. "I shall agree to your terms, then, Rory. You leave my mask alone, and I'll sweet-talk our unhappy visitor."

Frankly, I was still processing the news that Cass had been sneaking her manticore around the library during the Halloween party and nobody had noticed. I was trying to figure out how to tell Estelle when we walked into the lobby and found the ghost lurking beside the desk, wearing a woebegone expression.

"I convinced him to come downstairs," Estelle told me. "But I don't know how to keep him away from the shelves. Is Aunt Candace in the living quarters?"

"Yes, but there's something you should know—"

"Hello, Calvin," Aunt Candace said loudly. "My niece has insisted that I interrogate you."

I shot her an exasperated look. "That's not what I said. I thought my aunt might be able to prompt your memories of Halloween in case Dwight turns out to be innocent."

"Of course he's guilty," said Calvin. "He *said* he'd kill me."

"Did he?"

"He threatened to curse me, anyway," he amended. "What does it matter? I can't give evidence against him when the police can't actually see me."

Once again, he sounded a little too sure of himself. My suspicions rose. "If we don't find your killer, you can't move on, can you?"

"You've *found* my killer," he said. "All you're waiting for is a confession."

Definitely too sure of himself. "Say there's a one percent chance it isn't him. Who else might have been involved? How about that guy who found your body?"

"Terrance Linden," Estelle supplied. "That's his name."

"Terrance found me?" Calvin blinked. "That's weird. He left the party before I did."

"Did he, now?" Aunt Candace stepped closer to him, her notebook and pen floating up and down in midair. "Tell me more."

"There's nothing to tell," the ghost said. "I remember seeing Terrance leave the party alone, long before midnight. That's all."

"Are you sure it was him?" I wasn't certain how many

people at the party had been wearing masks covered with eyeballs, but he might not have been the only one.

"Positive," he said. "Also, he doesn't even live near the sea. What was he doing down there?"

"He doesn't?" I shared questioning looks with Estelle. If Terrance didn't live near the seafront, what had led to his walking down an alleyway and tripping over Calvin's body? Hadn't he said he was walking home at the time when Edwin had initially questioned him?

Maybe there was something to the ghost's words after all. It was also an excuse to drop in on Edwin and see if he'd had time to question Dwight yet—and to give Aunt Candace the chance to ask more questions of Calvin without any of the rest of us being around, if she stayed on topic, of course.

Estelle agreed, and we left for the police station. Once we were outside the library, I seized the chance to tell her about Cass's Halloween wanderings with the manticore.

"She did *what?*" she asked, aghast. "She's lucky that creature of hers didn't attack anyone."

"I know," I said. "I can't believe Aunt Candace knew and never mentioned it. Well, I *can* believe it, but when your mum finds out, she'll kill them both."

Estelle sucked in a breath. "Right. I'll talk to Cass when we get back."

"I can tell her," I offered. "Sorry. I know you didn't need that on your plate as well, but I figured you should know."

"No, I'm glad you told me." She released a sigh. "I might have to wait until after the ghost is gone to tell my mum, or else she might well be mad enough to send Cass and Aunt Candace to join him in the afterworld."

"Yeah... deal with the ghost first." And the Honeywoods.

I'd braced myself for another difficult session at the police station, but Edwin sat alone at his desk, a distinct air of satisfaction in his manner. Not a single member of Calvin's family was in sight..”

"Edwin." I halted in surprise. "How'd you get rid of the Honeywoods?"

I'd been starting to think that anything short of the trolls throwing them into the ocean wouldn't be enough to dissuade Cecilia from making his life a misery.

"I didn't," he replied. "They decided to go home."

What? "Without finding out what happened to Calvin?"

"They know what happened to him," he said. "Dwight is in custody. It's clean-cut."

It couldn't be that simple. "Has he confessed?"

"No, but he was all but certainly involved with Calvin's death."

"That might be true," I acknowledged. "But… Calvin's ghost said Terrance left the party long before the time when he found the body. He also said that Terrance doesn't live near the seafront."

"His ghost said that?"

"Yes, and he seemed quite sure of himself." Though I wasn't sure how much stock to put in the ghost's claims. Since Dwight was already in custody and Calvin thought him guilty, surely that ought to be enough for him to move on, yet still he remained in the library. Maybe he'd intended to wait until a direct confession, but if Dwight proved to be stubborn, that didn't bode well for the odds of the library staying in one piece.

And what if he isn't guilty, and Terrance was the one who killed him?

"Yes… I did think of bringing Terrance back in for further questioning," Edwin said. "However, I had no opportunity to question him further, after…"

"After the Honeywoods showed up," Estelle finished. "I'm not sure if the ghost was right, but I do wonder why

Terrance was wandering around the seafront in the middle of the night. Didn't he say he was on the way home when he tripped over the body?"

"Yes, he did." Edwin's jaw twitched. "His story never quite added up, truth be told. Very well. I will contact him."

"He doesn't sound that sure," I whispered to Estelle as we left.

"Can you blame Edwin for wanting a break?" Estelle said. "If I were him, I'd be planning a holiday. To the North Pole."

"Fair."

Weird. Why had the Honeywoods left town before the questioning? Maybe Edwin had taken extreme measures to stop them from interfering with their questioning Dwight and had one of his trolls throw Cecilia off the pier after all. Or maybe that was wishful thinking.

Estelle and I reached the square, and both of us came to a horrified halt. The library doors stood open, and a familiar blond silhouette filled the doorway.

Oh. Oh *no*.

Calvin Honeywood's family was in the library.

12

The Honeywoods had not left town after all. I should have known their sudden disappearance was too good to be true. Now, Cecilia Honeywood blocked the library's doorway, her strident voice drifting across the square. It sounded as if she was shrieking admonishments at whoever was at the front desk—meaning Aunt Adelaide—while the other Honeywoods formed a human shield around her.

"We have to rescue her," I whispered to Estelle. "Your mother, I mean."

"I think it's the ghost they want," she murmured back.

"Yeah." How had they found out he was in the library? Had someone told them? I'd thought nobody knew except for my family members. And Xavier, of course. And Edwin.

Estelle broke free of her trance first and ran across the square. I followed at speed and braced myself for the inevitable carnage.

"Excuse me," Estelle said in clear tones. "Is there a problem?"

"You." Cecilia whipped around. "Are you going to tell us why my brother is in your library?"

"I honestly have no idea." That was true, more or less, but her expression made it clear she didn't believe me. "He showed up out of nowhere with no memory of his death."

I'd privately hoped the last part would make it clear that he wasn't going to solve the problem of the inheritance, but she wasn't to be deterred. To Estelle, she said, "Well, I don't appreciate being deceived. You will find him for me at once."

"Of course," Estelle said politely. "May we get past?"

Cecilia huffed but shuffled a few inches to the side, and Estelle and I managed to squeeze past. Aunt Adelaide stood rigidly behind the front desk, and to no surprise, there was no sign of Calvin Honeywood's ghost. I did hear the distinct scratching noise of Aunt Candace's pen somewhere in the background. No doubt she was hiding out of the line of fire, but did I blame her at this point? This was exactly what Estelle and I had been trying to avoid.

"Come out and say hello, Calvin!" Cecilia bellowed. "We want to talk to you."

"Who told them he was here?" I asked, dropping my voice, as I edged closer to Aunt Adelaide, but Cecilia paid no more attention to us than she would a smudge of dirt on the floor.

"I don't know," she said out of the corner of her mouth. "Someone did, though."

"Edwin said they left town." I should have known better than to think they'd give up that easily, but the question of who'd given away his presence here at the library nagged at the back of my mind. Not Edwin… right?

"Calvin!" shouted Cecilia, and the other Honeywoods picked up her shout like an echo and repeated it until the library rang with the single word.

Yet no reply came from the ghost.

"Plainly, he doesn't want to answer," said Aunt Adelaide. "Now, please, I'll have to ask you to keep your voices down. You're in a library, remember?"

"You're holding my brother's ghost hostage!" Cecilia swooped upon her. "I'm within my rights to ignore your *rules*. Give him back."

"We aren't holding anyone hostage, Cecilia," Aunt Adelaide in steely calm tones. "I've spoken to Calvin myself, and he made it clear that he doesn't want to talk to you."

Cecilia went brick red. "You're abetting a criminal. He knows the money is rightfully mine, and he's withholding it. Calvin!"

She stalked past the desk and moved deeper into the library, ignoring Estelle's attempts to stop her.

"Where are you hiding?" Cecilia called out in her strident voice. "Calvin, where are you?"

Come on, Sylvester. Where was that owl? He didn't want the Honeywoods infesting the entire library, surely, but it was only a matter of time before Calvin knocked another shelf over and gave away his location.

"Can ghosts even be classed as criminals?" I muttered to Aunt Adelaide.

"No, and she's steering close to breaking the law herself." Aunt Adelaide hovered beside the desk, her expression conflicted as she watched Cecilia's fellow Honeywoods follow their leader past the research section. "I think I should call the police."

"Well, Edwin's free."

He'll be delighted. What had he expected, though? I wasn't sure whether to believe that he'd been vindictive enough to send the Honeywoods here, but he couldn't have expected them to have vanished from town outright.

There came a loud, familiar crashing noise from near the

Reading Corner. Cecilia veered in that direction like a hunting dog and gave a cry of triumph. "There you are."

Estelle ran to catch her up, and I followed fast on her heels, but Cecilia paid us no attention. She pulled out her wand as she walked, her cloak billowing around her legs, and a cluster of Honeywoods prevented me from reaching her before she pointed her wand at the shelves around the Reading Corner.

A large bookshelf flew upward, revealing Calvin's ghost hiding in the corner beside another collapsed shelf.

"Don't try to run from me!" Cecilia flicked her wand, sending the nearby shelves flying to either side so that Calvin had none left to conceal himself behind. I winced at the series of thuds when the books hit the floor after sliding off the shelves that Cecilia had callously tossed aside.

"Stop that at once!" Aunt Adelaide commanded. "You're damaging the library's property. If you continue, I'll call the police."

Cecilia ignored her outright, continuing to march on the cowering ghost. "Running away, are you? You think we'll forget you cheated us out of our money?"

"Leave me alone!" The ghost drifted sideways, heading for one of the open doors at the back of the library.

Cecilia followed. "You can't hide forever!"

Can't he? The library contained no end of hiding places, but I was more worried about what Sylvester would do when he finally snapped. For the second time in a day, the Reading Corner was in a state of chaos, books piled carelessly in heaps and shelves lying at crooked angles on the floor.

"That's enough!" Estelle shouted. "If you've damaged anything, you'll have to pay for it."

"Calvin can pay out of the inheritance he stole from us," Cecilia fired back at her. "Admit it, Calvin. You're a liar and a cheat."

"All right!" Calvin shouted. "All right, I did cheat. I forged the will."

Cecilia stopped midstride. "What did you say?"

"I used magic to alter our father's will," said the ghost, his gaze on his feet. "I wasn't supposed to inherit everything myself."

"I *knew* it!" Cecilia shouted, her triumphant cry echoed by the other Honeywoods. "That wasn't so hard, was it?"

Calvin said nothing. He drifted backwards, and as he did so, a tremor ran through the floor. Even the shelves that had already been knocked onto the floor wavered and fell over, shedding what remained of their contents.

"Now tell us where to find the real will," Cecilia went on. "Well?"

"It's gone," he mumbled. "I can't undo the spell now I'm dead, can I?"

"Nice try." She scoffed. "I won't accept your excuses. You'll come home with us to sort this out."

"No!" he said with sudden anger. "I'm not leaving the library. I can't leave."

"How dare you!" Cecilia lunged forward, stopping short of reaching him when an ominous shadow fell overhead, shaped distinctly like an owl. *There's Sylvester.*

"Oh boy." Estelle moved to my side and whispered, "Is it true, do you think? That he faked the will?"

"I think so." It must be. If he'd swiped his father's entire inheritance and then died without leaving any clear instructions as to who would get the money next, it was no wonder the other Honeywoods had been so determined to pin him down. "I don't know that Cecilia was responsible for this death."

"Yes, I thought he blamed Dwight."

Cecilia herself had gone oddly quiet. Her gaze rose upward to the owl, who'd perched on the balcony above. A breeze sprang up, as if someone had left a window open, and goose bumps sprang to my arms.

"You've gone too far," Aunt Adelaide said to Cecilia. "I'm going to have to ask you to leave. *Now.*"

Cecilia found her voice. "Not without our inheritance. Calvin, you're coming with us."

"No," Calvin whimpered. "I want to… leave."

Another shadow appeared behind him, this one larger, a blot of darkness that blurred out all the surrounding shelves. A figure appeared within, holding a scythe aloft.

All the air seemed to leave the library, and all of our eyes turned upon the forbidding figure. Without a word, the Grim Reaper swung the scythe downward, and Calvin Honeywood vanished into smoke.

13

———

Silence fell over the library in the wake of the Reaper's sudden appearance—then a scream, shrill and loud, and the thudding sound of footsteps as the Honeywoods fled across the lobby before the door slammed behind them.

Calvin Honeywood was gone. So was Cecilia, and with her departure brought a quietness so pronounced that you could have heard a page rustle from up on the top floor. The Grim Reaper stood in front of the wreckage of the Reading Corner's shelves with all the casualness of a movie hero walking away from an exploding building. Except most movie heroes weren't seven feet or more tall, entirely made out of shadows, and holding a giant scythe.

"What did you do that for?" I asked the Grim Reaper. "Calvin wasn't doing any harm."

Cecilia was, I thought, but there was zero chance he'd come here for the sole purpose of driving her off. Hell would freeze over first—literally.

"He asked me to banish him," he responded. "I can sense when a ghost desires to leave this realm behind. Besides, I would have expected you to thank me for getting him out of the library."

"That's not…" My thoughts struggled to catch up with me. He'd just… Reaped the guy's soul without even asking why Calvin had come back from the dead in the first place. "How are we supposed to solve his murder with him gone?"

"That," said the Grim Reaper, "is not my problem."

That figured. I hadn't thought he'd even cared that we had a ghost in the library, let alone cared enough for said ghost's well-being to put him out of his misery. Xavier hadn't mentioned spirits being able to call the Grim Reaper through the afterworld, but the desperation in Calvin's voice when he'd begged to leave had been stark.

He really was running away. And if he faked the will—

"Wait." I took a step forward, and the Grim Reaper vanished as if he'd never been here at all.

The darkness dissipated, and Sylvester fluttered down to land upon the wreckage of the upturned shelves. "Isn't anyone going to clean up this mess?"

"Yes." Estelle let out a shaky breath. "If you let us recover. Did the Grim Reaper… did he say that he sensed the ghost *wanted* to leave?"

"That or Cecilia's yelling reached him in the afterworld somehow and woke him from a nap."

I spoke lightly, but my heart dropped somewhere into the vicinity of the vampire's basement. Yes, the Honeywoods had gone—the one silver lining was that the Grim Reaper had scared them off—but that didn't mean they'd *stay* gone. There was no way to banish a *living* person, and now there was zero hope of Calvin unearthing a will that would get them what they wanted.

"Well, that's them taken care of," Sylvester said cheerfully. "I was debating dropping a cabinet on that Cecilia's head, but I suppose a scythe is the next best thing."

"Why did you let them trash the place first?" I gestured at the pile of upended shelves. "And the ghost? Couldn't you have scared him off from the start rather than waiting for him to spend days wreaking havoc?"

"Spirits are part of the afterworld, not the library, you turnip" was his reply.

"Unfortunately, he's right." Aunt Adelaide approached us. "That said, it'll be a lot easier to tidy up without a ghost constantly knocking things over."

True. The ghost's disappearance would solve at least one of our problems, but the question remained of who'd told Cecilia he was present in the library in the first place. Not Edwin, surely. He might have been desperate to get rid of the Honeywoods, but he wouldn't have gone that far, right?

I mulled over the possibilities while I helped Aunt Adelaide and Estelle clean up the mess of the Reading Corner. Mercifully, no books had been damaged in the fall, though Aunt Adelaide declared in no uncertain terms that the Honeywoods were banned from the library for life.

While I was sorting books into piles, I spied Aunt Candace walking behind the Reading Corner's shelves with her notebook and pen floating behind her.

"There you are," I called to her. "Want to come and help?"

"Why, you're doing such an astounding job that I wouldn't want to interfere." She sauntered away, humming under her breath.

"Why is she so cheerful?" Estelle muttered. "I'd have thought she'd be sad the ghost's gone."

"Same." Where was she going? The fourth floor? Wait… come to think of it, with the ghost no longer here, there was no reason for the guardian to prevent me from getting into the fourth-floor corridor and retrieving the Book of Questions, if that was indeed where it had been all along.

Not that I had a solid question to ask the book either. Its

knowledge solely encompassed the library, nothing more, so the book was very unlikely to be able to tell me why the ghost had shown up in the library in the first place or the identity of his murderer. Sylvester's earlier comment meant those issues might be beyond the scope of the Book of the Questions. No, the answers, if any existed, lay outside of the library.

When we'd finished tidying up, I was in dire need of some fresh air. The shelves' second collapse in as many days had stirred up enough dust that we were coughing with every breath, and there was still a distinct lack of any visitors to the library.

"Should I tell Edwin the ghost has gone?" I suggested to Estelle between coughs. "I can also see if he's managed to talk to Dwight yet."

"Are you sure that isn't where the Honeywoods went?"

Good point. Edwin would be immensely displeased at that turn of events, though if the Honeywoods were indeed back at the police station, there was a chance I might be able to find out who'd spilled the beans about Calvin's location. Yes, anyone who'd visited the library in the last few days would have glimpsed some of the destruction, but the only people who'd known a ghost was responsible were those I'd told myself.

"I'll risk it." I made for the door. "If they aren't there, someone ought to tell him the ghost's gone anyway."

"Good luck," said Estelle.

I walked out into the wind and rain and crossed the square to the seafront. Thanks to Estelle's warning, I already half expected the inevitable moment when I turned the corner and heard the strident noise of Cecilia's voice drifting out of the police station. *Here we go again.*

When I entered, Cecilia whipped around to face me. "You. Have you come to apologise for terrorising my family?"

"Only if you apologise for damaging *my* family's property." I hadn't known the words were going to escape before they did. They were born of pent-up frustration at both her and the situation in general. "What are you doing here?"

"We were just leaving," she said haughtily. "We're done with this town. You've made your position clear."

That still wasn't an apology, but I hadn't expected one. Edwin looked on hopefully as she made a motion towards the door.

"Who told you Calvin's ghost was in the library?" I blurted. "It wasn't anyone in my family."

"That young man did," Cecilia said. "He was on his way to that strange pub down the road."

"The Black Dog?" Who did she mean? I looked questioningly at Edwin, but his expression showed nothing but relief as the group of Honeywoods traipsed out of the police station.

When Cecilia finally vanished in a cloud of perfume, Edwin's mouth twitched as if he was fighting a smile. "There's that, then."

"I guess so." I'd quite forgotten why I'd originally come here; before I could gather my thoughts, Edwin cleared his throat.

"Well, Aurora?" he said. "Have you satisfied your curiosity?"

"I didn't know they'd be here." I shook my thoughts back into line. "I... I guess you know the ghost has gone. Do you know who Cecilia was talking about? Who told her he was in the library?"

"No." He didn't elaborate. "Was that all?"

"Ah..." I backtracked. "Calvin Honeywood admitted that he forged the paperwork for his father's will and wasn't supposed to inherit everything himself. Did Cecilia tell you that too?"

"Yes, she did," he said. "I made it clear that it's beyond our abilities to help deal with the problem of this inheritance and that they'll have to find someone else closer to home. That's all I can do."

"You don't think they killed him?" I asked.

"No," he said. "I have yet to question Dwight, for reasons that I'm sure you've guessed."

"And Terrance?" I asked. "Did you find out why he walked all the way to the seafront and happened to fall over a body?"

Edwin's jaw twitched. "No, because people keep showing up here and keeping me from doing my job."

I flushed. "Sorry. I just wanted to make sure you knew the ghost had gone, and… and that someone told the Honeywoods he was hiding in the library. We had to ban the whole family from coming back after the damage they did."

"I don't expect they'll be returning to Ivory Beach at all," he said. "As for who told them, your family has a certain knack for drawing attention. So did that Calvin Honeywood, come to that."

"I wouldn't have minded knowing why he came back from the dead in the first place." That was Xavier's area, though, and I might need to wait for his boss to calm down before I paid him another visit.

Leaving Edwin to recover from the ordeal, I walked back to the library and found it blessedly free of Honeywoods but also empty of any patrons.

"You look like Sylvester put a dead mouse in your coffee," Aunt Candace said to me as I walked into the lobby. "You should be happy that awful coven has gone."

"How'd you know they left?"

"Instinct," she said smugly. "Now, if you ask me, we have a great excuse to throw another party."

"Definitely not." Estelle walked over to join me. "Have they really gone, Rory?"

"Yeah, they were just leaving when I got to the police station," I replied. "Cecilia, though… She said a young man told her to come here to find Calvin. No idea who it was."

"Weird." Her brow wrinkled. "I guess there were a few people who might have seen the ghost."

"Not that many." Calvin himself had seen to that.

"Oh, the whole town will be talking about it for a week," Aunt Candace said. "Now, if you'll excuse me. I have a book to write."

"It doesn't feature the Honeywood Coven, does it?" Estelle asked suspiciously.

"What do you take me for?" She grinned. "It's about a group of witches called the Honeybane Coven who turn into bats."

"As long as Cecilia doesn't find out." I turned towards the stairs. "I'm going to see if the Book of Questions has turned up." *And if the guardian has calmed down,* I added silently, not wanting to give Aunt Candace any further ideas.

I walked up three storeys until I came to the third floor. There, I found Cass peering out of the doorway to the Magical Creatures Division.

"Is it over?" she asked.

"No. Yes." I backtracked, unsure whether now was the right time to bring up the manticore, or if I should leave that to Aunt Adelaide and Estelle instead. "I mean, the part with the ghost is over. We still don't know who killed him."

"So? That's Edwin's job."

"Yes, but I'd like to know why the ghost ended up in the library in the first place." I nodded in the general direction of the fourth floor. "I'd also like to know why the Book of Questions disappeared."

"I thought it was obvious that the guardian was protecting it from the ghost." She reached into a pocket and pulled out the large blank-covered book. "I got it back. You're welcome."

"Oh. Thanks." Surprised, I took the Book of Questions from her. "The guardian's back to normal, is it?"

"I didn't see it, but I assume so." She made to close the door to the Magical Creatures Division.

I caught the door in my hand. "Wait."

"What?" She met my gaze defiantly, and my nerve fled. Did I really want to start an argument about the ethics of her sneaking around the library with a manticore in tow on Halloween when she'd just done me a massive favour?

"Nothing." Releasing the door, I lifted the book and flipped it open. "I wish to enter the Forbidden Room."

The pages expanded to fill my vision, and I toppled forward, headfirst, into a room with walls as blank as the book's pages. I landed on my front soundlessly and breath-lessly, my elbows sinking into soft carpet. For a moment, I simply stared at the floor. *Ah... should probably have thought of a question first.*

I rose upright slowly and scanned the blank-walled room.

"Well?" said the owl's voice. "Are you going to stare clue-lessly into space forever?"

"No." Scrambling, I asked the first question that came to mind. "Why did the ghost of Calvin Honeywood appear in the library?"

"You'll have to ask him, not me."

"I can't do that, can I?" Had I wasted my question? That's what I got for coming in here without a plan.

"Yes, you can."

The floor collapsed. I fell into oblivion and landed on my back, this time painfully, the breath flying from my lungs. The ceiling danced above my head, and it took a moment to recognise my surroundings. The room had dropped me beside the front desk, which at least saved me from walking downstairs, but my back felt like the owl had kicked me with one of his talons. *Ow.*

A bewildered Estelle peered down at my face. "Rory, are you okay?"

"I think so." Righting myself, I picked up the Book of Questions. "Cass managed to get this back from the fourth-floor corridor. Unfortunately, it wasn't much help."

"What question did you ask?"

"I wanted to know why the ghost appeared here when this wasn't where he died," I said. "The room, or Sylvester, told me to ask the ghost, which is about as useless a response as you can get."

Estelle blinked. "What? Did the room mean for you to summon him back?"

"Summon the ghost?" Was that even possible at this point? Even if it was, I couldn't say I relished the notion of bringing Calvin Honeywood's destructive spirit back into the library—and that was assuming the Grim Reaper didn't come back for an encore too.

"I meant Xavier," she said hastily. "Not you. He can get into the afterworld, even the parts that are off-limits to the rest of us. He won't need to be in the library to contact the ghost either."

I raised a brow. "Would his boss like that idea?"

"Probably not," she acknowledged. "Also, I think we could all use a break from the Honeywoods for a long while—all of them."

"True." I pulled out my phone and scrolled to Xavier's number. "I don't want to see the ghost again either. I only asked the room a question because… well. I was going to mention Cass's manticore excursion, but I figured I should leave that to your mum."

"Right." She pressed a hand to her forehead. "I forgot to tell her."

"Tell me what?" Aunt Adelaide walked into view, and her gaze landed on the book in my hands. "Oh good. You found it."

"It was upstairs on the fourth floor, like we thought." Estelle took in a breath. "Cass found it, but Rory couldn't get a straight answer on why the ghost showed up in the library. I can try asking why the ghost freaked out the library so badly, but... I don't know that Sylvester would want to answer that either."

"No, he wouldn't," said the owl from the top shelf.

"That saves time." Estelle faced her mother. "Ah, I should tell you about what Cass did."

As she began to speak, someone knocked on the library's door. My heart leapt. *Xavier.* Nobody else would knock on the door during opening hours, and when I opened the door, even the sound of Estelle explaining Cass's misdemeanours faded into the background.

I wrapped Xavier in a hug. "I was going to come and see you, but I figured your boss would object."

"I managed to get away," he said. "I'm sorry he banished the ghost."

"It's hardly your fault," I protested. "You didn't ask him to. Besides, I think everyone is glad he's gone."

"I could have tried harder to stop him."

"Cecilia Honeywood caused more damage than the ghost did, but she's gone too." I took his hand. "Want to go for a walk?"

Out of the corner of my eye, I saw Aunt Adelaide staring at Estelle in horror and discerned that Estelle had just broken the news of Cass's excursion on Halloween. As well as my desire to get away from the fallout, a far more significant part of me craved aloneness with Xavier. Besides, if he *could* talk to Calvin's ghost on the other side, I didn't want to drag my family into it again.

"Sure." Xavier slid his hand into mine, and we walked out of the library, leaving the sound of Aunt Adelaide's shout of *"She did what?"* in our wake. "Ah… is your aunt okay?"

"Estelle just told her what Cass did on Halloween," I explained. "Turns out she sneaked the manticore out for a walk while everyone was at the party."

He winced. "She's lucky it didn't attack anyone."

"Yeah, I thought that too," I said. "I only found out because Aunt Candace gave the game away. Now I feel bad for telling tales myself because Cass helped me earlier. She got the Book of Questions back from the fourth-floor corridor."

"The… book?"

"Oh, right, I didn't have time to tell you." I summarised the now-resolved mystery of the missing book and the guardian's bizarre behaviour. "It was all the ghost, in the end. Not Aunt Candace's mask."

"Sorry." He squeezed my hand. "I missed a lot. My boss… I'd like to think he's feeling a little remorseful about banishing that ghost, but I have my doubts."

"It was the ghost who called your boss in the first place," I said. "I didn't even know that was possible, but that's what he said."

"If a spirit is desperate enough, they put out signals we Reapers can sense," he said. "Calvin must have been really freaked out by his sister's ranting."

"She did get him to admit he faked their dad's will and shouldn't have got the inheritance," I said. "That might have done it."

He gave a low whistle. "Wow. Is that why they left town? To find the real will?"

"He said it doesn't exist," I replied. "He altered the will using magic, and now he's dead, he can't do anything about it. I think Cecilia reluctantly concluded that Edwin can't resolve that one."

"That and she's probably mentally scarred from seeing my boss Reap someone's soul."

"Couldn't have happened to a nicer person." I managed a smile. "Some of us see that kind of thing more often than others."

"Yeah." His smile faded. "I wish…"

"Don't say you wish I didn't have to. I don't mind. Anything's worth it with you. Almost anything," I amended. "I could do without your boss holding the threat of him cutting off contact with you over my head."

"That won't happen," he said. "Never. Also, with the Honeywoods gone, we can go back to the Black Dog without them hanging around."

"Unless they're the murderers," I added. "That's the thing. Edwin's so relieved that they left town that he's dismissed them as suspects, but it sounds like they had twice the reason to murder Calvin now he's admitted to forging the paper-work on his dad's will."

"I thought Dwight was the main suspect."

"So did I." I shrugged one shoulder. "I feel like we missed the chance to find out why Calvin came back from the dead in the first place. I… well, I tried to ask the Book of Questions, but Sylvester just told me to ask the ghost."

"Ask the *ghost?*" He blinked. "Doesn't the book—I mean Sylvester—know he's gone?"

"Yes." I paused. "He implied you could call him back from the afterworld."

His expression darkened. "Now, *that'll* have consequences from my boss. Would it really be worth it?"

"I guess not." My sense of unease remained, though. "Oh, and Cecilia said that some man told her to find Calvin's ghost in the library, but she wasn't very specific."

"What man?"

"Someone on his way to the Black Dog pub this morning." Which was kind of an odd time of day to go to the pub, now that I thought about it. "That's all she said."

"We can go there," he offered. "And ask. If it'll make you feel better."

I didn't have any better ideas at hand, so we angled our steps towards the seafront. This time, we veered past the police station and into the pub. It was quiet during the day, though a few people sat at tables, eating lunch, no doubt happy to get out of the cold sea air.

Xavier walked over to speak to the bartender. "Excuse me. This is an odd question, but did someone come here alone earlier this morning? A young man?"

"Might have to be more specific," said the bartender. "Alone, you say? This morning... Huh, do you mean Terrance... What's his name? Lindon?"

Terrance. "Does he come here a lot?"

"Fairly often," he said. "He used to meet with that wizard at least once a week."

"Who?" My suspicions multiplied. "What wizard?"

"The one who works in construction. I forget his name."

Dwight. "Did they come here the night of the Halloween party?"

"Funny you should say that," he said. "I was working until closing time, and I saw Terrance hanging around outside. I think he'd have come in if it'd been open."

Hmm.

"Thanks for the help." Xavier took my hand in his, and we left the pub once again.

When we were outside, we both looked at one another.

"Seems fishy," I commented. "What were those two meeting for?"

"No idea. Edwin said he was going to contact him, right? Terrance, I mean."

"Yes, because he doesn't live anywhere near the seafront," I said. "Which means he had no good reason to be here the night of the party when he tripped over Calvin's body. Let alone if he was meeting with the other main suspect."

No. It was definitely time to have another word with Terrance.

14

Edwin must have had a change of heart. When we entered the police station, he wore an expression of contrition. "I apologise for how I spoke to you earlier, Rory. I'm sure you know how frustrating that woman is."

"She's gone now." I nodded to Xavier. "But I'm pretty sure the person who told her that Calvin's ghost was in the library was Terrance Lindon."

"We also found out that Terrance has been frequently meeting with Dwight Keaton in the Black Dog pub," Xavier added. "Including on the night of the Halloween party, though the pub wasn't open at the time."

Edwin's mouth pressed into a thin line. "Is that so?"

"Dwight himself might confirm it," I added. "If he's honest. Have you spoken to him?"

"Yes..." Edwin exhaled a sigh. "The trouble is I let Dwight go."

My heart missed a beat. "You did what?"

"He had an alibi," he replied. "Multiple people can confirm he hadn't left the party at the time of the murder."

"Terrance was waiting for him, though." Had he stayed at the party to divert suspicion or to make sure Terrance took the fall for his crime? Or had Terrance himself been oblivious to being manipulated? "The guy who works at the pub has no reason to lie to us, I wouldn't have thought."

"I'm sure you're right, Rory, but Dwight gave extensive evidence that he was at the library at the time of Calvin's death, and several witnesses confirmed it."

"He didn't need to be near Calvin at the time to be responsible for his murder." We'd established that from the start. "And Terrance?"

"Speaking to him was my next plan," he said. "And yes, fine. You can both come with me."

I blinked in surprise. "Seriously?"

"Yes, if you don't make me regret it." He rose from his seat. "Since you have the word of the ghost that he doesn't live near where he stumbled over Calvin's body, you can tell Terrance yourselves."

And that he was hanging around the Black Dog pub. Edwin must really feel bad for driving me off earlier if he was actually letting Xavier and me help, though I didn't blame him for being irked by Cecilia's constant presence at the police station. Perhaps he'd initially thought I'd sent her back here after she trashed the library.

"I hope she and the others are really gone for good," I murmured to Xavier as we walked behind Edwin out of the police station. "We don't need to run into them on the way to Terrance's house."

"No. They must have realised the police of Ivory Beach aren't equipped to deal with a will from someone in a different town," he said. "Probably, they've gone to pester the police department in their own home instead."

"Pity for them."

The silence between the three of us as we walked wasn't

quite as awkward as when I'd gone with Edwin to speak to Dwight, but it was pretty close. I tried to make conversation a couple of times, but Edwin replied in monosyllables, and Xavier seemed content to stay quiet. Since he was a Reaper, nothing fazed him.

Eventually, we reached a terraced house that looked a little like someone had tried to copy Dwight's exterior décor by hiring someone with a fraction of the talent. The walls were slightly curved inward, while the pointed-hat-shaped roof was missing several tiles in a pattern that was evidently supposed to look aesthetic but also made me wonder what he did when it rained.

Edwin knocked, and the door swung inward. I almost didn't recognise Terrance without the eyeball mask he'd been wearing the last time I'd seen him. When he set eyes on Xavier, he flinched. "Edwin. Why is the Reaper here?"

"I asked him to come with me," said Edwin. "And I'm going to ask *you* to come and answer some questions."

Terrance didn't move. "Didn't I already answer all your questions the other night?"

"New information has come to light," said Edwin. "My first question concerns this." He gestured at Terrance's house. "In your initial report, you were going home when you found Calvin's body at the seafront. Plainly, you live in the opposite direction."

Terrance flushed. "I was taking a longer route. I had an errand I needed to run."

"In the middle of the night?" Edwin paused and then ploughed on. "Did it involve meeting up with Dwight Keaton?"

Terrance's flush deepened. "Who told you that?"

"A witness." Edwin eyed him. "Well? Is it true?"

"I didn't meet anyone."

"But you planned to," Edwin pressed. "It wouldn't have

been the first time you met him. I'm told you've been frequently meeting at the Black Dog pub."

"That's not illegal." Terrance backtracked. "Wait. It's not like that. It was nothing to do with… I mean, he wanted to interview me as a replacement for his last business partner, but they'd already stopped working together by then."

"Meaning Calvin Honeywood?" Edwin asked in a tight voice. "Calvin was his past business partner, correct?"

"I—yes." Terrance dropped his gaze. "Like I said, they'd already fallen out."

"Am I to understand you were going to meet with him in the middle of the night, during the party?" Edwin pressed.

"We talked at the party," he clarified. "And… we were going to meet at the pub afterwards, but we both lost track of time and forgot it would be closed by midnight."

Edwin's lips pressed together. Plainly, he didn't buy that excuse, and neither did I, for that matter. "When did these meetings start? Before Calvin's death?"

"Yes, but they'd already stopped working together as business partners," said Terrance. "I didn't have anything to do with what happened to him. To Calvin."

"Really." Edwin was silent for a moment. "I think you should come with me to the police station so we can talk in more detail."

Terrance gulped. "I'm innocent."

"We'll see." Edwin beckoned. "Come on."

Just then, a large shadow fell over all our heads, and my heart plummeted. *Not again.*

Terrance gasped, while Edwin went equally still when the shadowy figure materialised behind Xavier with his scythe held in both hands.

Xavier swivelled towards him, his jaw tight. "What are you doing here? There are no souls to Reap."

"This man," said the Grim Reaper, "is not what he claims to be."

"What does that mean?" Xavier looked back at Terrance, his face mirroring my own confusion. "He's as human as Rory is."

"No."

"What does that mean?" Xavier took a step closer and lowered his voice so that only we and the Grim Reaper could hear. "If this is about Rory, I've already made my position clear. This situation isn't relevant to you. Didn't you already banish Calvin's ghost?"

"Yes," he replied. "However, there's someone else who needs to be taken care of."

"Terrance is alive." Wasn't he? He sure looked normal to me and scared half to death too—for good reason because of the close proximity of the Grim Reaper's scythe.

"For now," said the Grim Reaper, in ominous tones. "Come and speak to me if you want the truth."

He vanished into smoke. As the darkness faded, Terrance fell to his knees, his entire body shaking.

"What was that about?" Edwin recovered first, though his face was still ashen. "You—where are you going?"

Xavier had turned away, but I ran after him. "I don't care what your boss says. I'm coming with you."

I grabbed his arm tightly, and Xavier went still for a heartbeat. Then the afterworld closed in, masking the street around us.

A moment later, we reappeared in the doorway of the Reaper's house. The Grim Reaper stood imperiously in front of us, his forbidding figure towering over my head. "Breaking the rules again, I see."

"You *told* us to come and see you," I said. "I got the impression it's urgent. What's the problem with Terrance?"

"Not him."

"You just implied you were going to Reap his soul." I looked at Xavier, perplexed. "What *is* going on? Is it to do with why you keep getting dragged off to run errands?"

"You overstep, Aurora." To Xavier, he added, "Now do you understand why I warned you about her? No amount of access to your life is ever going to be enough for her. She'll keep wheedling her way in until the Reaper's secrets are laid bare before her and are exposed in her mind for anyone to snatch."

"You think I'm going to give you away to the vampires." *That* was the problem? "Okay, first of all, if you have a problem with me, I'd really prefer it if you said it to my face. Secondly, I have an anti-mind-reading potion straight from Evangeline herself. I have no intention of letting the vampires into my thoughts."

"Did you believe the same when you got yourself captured and had to enlist the aid of a certain device that belongs to the Reapers to request Xavier's aid?" he enquired. "A device that he should never have given to you in the first place?"

Heat crept up my neck, but I stood my ground. "It wasn't *your* secrets the vampires were after."

No, they wanted the library's secrets, but something had held them back—a shadow shaped like the guardian, which had prevented them from seeing into my inmost thoughts. Not that I wanted to tell *him* that. It wasn't any more his business than it was the Founders'.

"Nevertheless," said the Grim Reaper, "you both endangered the Reapers with your actions, and I've been working to the utmost to fix the damage."

"That's untrue," Xavier said. "The actions of a few wayward wizards on Samhain had nothing to do with Rory. People always try to mess with the afterworld on that night. You and I both know that."

"I don't care what happened on Samhain," I interjected. "I'm not trying to steal your secrets. I don't even care what you Reapers do in your free time. Listen—"

"You *should* care what happened on Samhain," said the Grim Reaper.

My heart skipped a beat. "Why? Because of Calvin Honeywood?"

"I'm guessing so." Xavier turned to his boss. "I might remind you that Calvin's ghost decided to haunt Rory's home for a reason, and I'm as curious to know why as she is."

He doesn't know. He'd been running around, cleaning up after people who'd decided to contact the dead on Samhain, but the boss hadn't even told Xavier himself the truth.

"On the night of Samhain, someone in this very town was meddling with the afterworld." The Grim Reaper fixed me with one of his empty stares. "Yes. Someone inside Ivory Beach summoned a ghost."

I didn't get it. "Not Calvin Honeywood. He wasn't dead yet."

"I didn't sense anything," Xavier put in. "Why didn't you tell me?"

"I hoped you'd be paying enough attention to notice," he said, "but you've been distracted from your duties for a long time."

The slightest flush touched Xavier's face. "You were deliberately trying to mislead me. You took me out of town on purpose, didn't you?"

"I humoured you when you wanted to go up north to help your other Reaper friend, but that is no excuse to neglect your duties here." The Grim Reaper's tone remained unforgiving. "Nevertheless, I was able to sense a surge of energy in the afterworld that indicated a spirit was summoned, and that spirit committed a great crime against the living."

"A crime?" Comprehension dawned on me. "Calvin…"

"The person who killed him was a ghost," Xavier said suddenly. "The ghost of—what family member he inherited from? Or shouldn't have inherited from?"

"His father. He faked the will." My heart began to race. "Someone summoned his ghost on purpose. The Honeywoods... No. They don't live in Ivory Beach. They weren't here."

"I care not who was summoned," said the Grim Reaper. "My priority is punishing those responsible. That man you were speaking to was involved but not the perpetrator."

"Not Terrance." I glanced at Xavier as more pieces fell into place. "Dwight? He was already taken in for questioning. He's been the main suspect all along, more or less, but he refused to admit anything, and the police let him go."

"Dwight Keaton had an alibi, but if a ghost is the one who committed the murder, and he summoned it... There'll be proof somewhere. In his house, perhaps," Xavier said.

"Likely, yes," said the Grim Reaper.

"And?" Xavier went on. "Are you going to let me search for the proof without hovering over my shoulder? If I'm to prove I'm trustworthy, I'll have to be allowed to do things alone."

"You aren't alone." His stare landed on me. It was amazing how he could project such disdain without any visible facial features.

"Rory has a right to be involved in this too," Xavier protested. "Dwight committed murder on the night of her family's event. He didn't summon the ghost in the library, but I imagine his actions had a knock-on effect and are responsible for Calvin's ghost ending up inside her family's home."

"Exactly," I said. "I'll stay out of Xavier's way, if you want, but you're going to have to trust him again."

"You won't stay out of his way," said the Grim Reaper. "You're incapable of it."

I had to concede that that was accurate enough. "I did tell you from the start, remember? Xavier and I are together. If you don't accept that, you're breaking our original agreement. Using that stone to ask for his help in a time of crisis is hardly worth this much fuss."

"And every moment we waste, Dwight might be getting away," Xavier added. "Let us search his house. We'll find what we need."

"And if he *has* left town?" asked the Grim Reaper. "What then?"

"I can…"

"Xavier can track him," I finished. "Don't look at me like that. You know perfectly well that Xavier can find him in a fraction of the time it would take anyone else to. Why should he not use that ability to make his life easier?"

"Taking a human with you is—"

"It went perfectly fine the last few times I did it," Xavier interjected. "I recently met a Reaper who used his scythe as a hat stand. I'm hardly the worst offender."

Huh? I'd have to get that story out of him later. For now, I said, "Dwight and Terrance broke the Reapers' rules themselves when they summoned the dead. Isn't that something you're supposed to deal out punishment for?"

"She's right," Xavier said, "and they might have summoned other ghosts too. People who meddle with the afterworld rarely get it right on the first go."

"That is correct," the Grim Reaper said. "Fine. Do what you will."

We'd won the argument by some miracle. Maybe there was hope left after all, but I wouldn't push my luck.

I'd intended to leave the house via the door, but Xavier took my hand and pulled me into the afterworld, straight in front of his boss's face.

An instant later, we both landed in front of Dwight's

mismatched house. Thankfully, the Grim Reaper hadn't come with us.

"Were you just trying to annoy him?" I asked. "Because I'm not sure that was wise."

"He owes me for deceiving me on purpose. Anyway, this is much faster than walking." Xavier eyed the tall, crooked walls and hat-shaped roof in front of us. "Is this what Terrance's house was trying to imitate?"

"I think so," I said. "He and Dwight both work in magical construction. They were going to be business partners after Dwight's falling-out with Calvin."

"Ah." He trod closer and peered through the window, but the curtains were drawn tight. "I can't sense anyone in there."

"He's gone?" I approached the door, apprehensive. "When did you meet a Reaper who used his scythe as a hat stand?"

"Last week," he said. "When I went up north to help Maura."

"Oh." It'd slipped my mind that Maura had stayed in touch. The other Reaper had recently visited town while investigating a thorny problem from up north where she lived, and evidently Xavier had gone to help her in person. "I guess that didn't help your boss's mood."

"No," he said, "but I think he's starting to see sense. We just need to find that proof."

He glided forward, through the afterworld, and I took his hand again. There was no need to use a front door while in the company of a Reaper, and an instant later, we both landed in a hallway that was just as eccentrically designed as the outside of the house. The walls were curved and hollow like the inside of a tree, while doors branched off like… well, branches.

Xavier raised his head and paced ahead of me, as though sensing something I couldn't.

"Can you sniff out weirdness in the afterworld like a dog following a scent?" I asked.

He gave me an amused look. "If you want to use that analogy. There's definitely something off in here but no living people."

Xavier nudged a door inward. The room on the other side at first appeared to be a normal study, but when he walked in, I glimpsed the outline of a circle on the floor drawn in chalk.

He sniffed. "That's sage."

"Isn't that ghost repellent?"

"It also protects the person doing the summoning from whatever's in there." He indicated the circle. "He summoned something inside that boundary."

"The ghost?"

He shook his head. "Can't tell. Whatever it is, it's not in the house. It'd have sensed me by now."

My skin crawled. Now he'd mentioned it, a *presence* seemed to linger around the circle, traces of shadows that didn't belong to any of the objects in the room.

Xavier reached for my hand and gave it a squeeze.

"I think this is proof enough for Edwin," he said. "We'll let him know."

The afterworld closed around us like a cool embrace.

15

We landed in front of the police station this time and saw that Edwin had just taken Terrance inside and handed him over to the troll guards. As for Dwight, though… he must have left town as soon as he'd escaped the police's clutches. Edwin, focused on dealing with the Honeywoods, would have overlooked him.

"I should have guessed," I murmured. "Dwight must have known we'd come looking for proof as soon as we made the connection. He's got to have known your Reaper abilities clued you in to what he did."

"Yeah." Xavier strode ahead of me into the police station. "Edwin. Dwight has left town."

Next to him, Terrance jumped violently. "What do you want this time, Reaper?"

"You thought I wouldn't figure out what your ally did?" Xavier asked chillingly. "Edwin, we found evidence at Dwight's house that he summoned a spirit. I believe that spirit killed Calvin Honeywood."

"I didn't do it!" Terrance protested. "It was all him."

"I know both you and Dwight conspired to kill Calvin together," Xavier corrected him. "Didn't you?"

"And now Dwight's run off and left you to take the fall." I looked at Edwin. "Does that sound plausible to you?"

"It wasn't my idea," Terrance blurted. "Dwight was the mastermind."

"That's as good as a confession," Xavier said.

Edwin, recovering from our sudden arrival, glared at Xavier and then at me. "You broke into Dwight's house?"

"I'm a Reaper," Xavier said simply. "I had reason to believe Dwight was meddling with the afterworld, and my instincts turned out to be correct. Moreover, he appears to have left town to escape the consequences of his actions, and he's taken whatever he summoned with him."

"I wouldn't follow him." Terrance changed tack. "He's dangerous."

"I have no reason to fear the living *or* the dead," Xavier said. "I'll find him."

Edwin's glare melted off his face, and now he looked slightly faint. "You… you'll bring him straight here, I take it?"

"Not if my boss wants a word with him first." Xavier reached for my arm. "Ready?"

Not in the slightest. Dwight was dangerous, undeniably, but my place was at Xavier's side. That had never been in doubt.

I nodded and slid my hand into his, then we stepped through the afterworld again. Xavier raised his head northward, a frown on his mouth, but the darkness surrounding us was impenetrable. I could only trust in him to know where he was going and to be able to track Dwight on the other side of the darkness.

Abruptly, Xavier let go of my hand. I stumbled out of the darkness as a huge shape loomed overhead—taller than a Reaper, taller than any creature I'd seen—and Xavier lifted his scythe to shield us from the dark shape.

The darkness resolved itself into a huge, towering monster, its jaws agape to reveal slavering teeth. Shaggy fur covered its body. No, not fur but shadow thicker than any I'd seen. Its vast paws were planted on the grassy hillside while Dwight stood next to the monster he'd summoned. The beast dwarfed him, but he showed no signs of fear.

His mouth twitched into a smile. "I knew you'd follow me, Reaper."

"What did you do?" asked Xavier. "You summoned that thing in your *house*? And then you let it escape the summoning circle? It might have killed someone."

"Stay away from me, Reaper," he warned him. "This beast is more dangerous to you than it is to me."

"Who told you that?" Xavier narrowed his eyes. "For that matter, where did you learn to summon it?"

"I don't think you're in any position to make demands of me, Reaper." Despite his bravado, Dwight stumbled downhill from Xavier's advance, keeping a wary eye on the scythe in his hands.

"It's not a demand. It's a question," said Xavier. "If you have an accomplice, they're in as much danger as you are. The afterworld doesn't forget those who meddle without understanding its workings."

Dwight scoffed. "You're talking absolute nonsense. The afterworld is a place. It doesn't have feelings."

He's wrong. I'd freely admit that I'd hardly begun to understand the afterworld myself, but I'd spent long enough in the library to know that a place could have its own sentience, its own will.

The beast at Dwight's side let out a rumbling growl. Xavier took a step back, lifting his scythe defensively in front of the pair of us again.

"Do you really have control over that creature?" he enquired. "I have my doubts."

The monster locked its eyes on Xavier and released a roar that was far louder than any creature's I'd heard before. I held my hands over my ears, my head throbbing with the noise, and raised my gaze to Dwight. The colour had drained from his face, and with one last terrified look at the monster, he turned heel and bolted.

As he ran down the hillside, the beast turned on the last remaining target—us. At the same instant, Xavier grabbed my arm, pulling me into the afterworld.

"What—?" I lowered my hands from my ears, my head still vibrating from the aftermath of the monster's roar. "What *is* that thing?"

"A hellbeast," Xavier whispered. "They… Well, they usually feed on the dead. I guess that answers the question as to how he got rid of the ghost of Calvin's father after he'd committed the murder."

"They feed on the *dead*?" My mouth fell open. "Is that why Calvin came into the library? He was running away?"

"Likely, yes." He swore softly. "I doubt Dwight had the knowledge to banish the monster once he'd summoned it, so he had to keep it contained until he got scared that I'd find the evidence."

"Why is it obeying him?" I murmured back. "How did he figure out how to summon it in the first place?"

"That, I don't know." He sucked in a breath. "Either he got lucky… or someone helped him."

Someone… like another Reaper?

"Is it really dangerous to Reapers?" I asked.

"Not as much as ghosts." He hefted his scythe again. "It can travel through the afterworld too. Rory, stay behind me."

A great tremor rang through the darkness surrounding us. Xavier took my arm and pulled me out of the darkness, and we landed further down the hillside we'd left behind. As the shadows receded, I saw Dwight's figure in the distance, running away.

"We can't let him escape," I said. "Not again."

"I know," Xavier said, "but that monster—"

He cut off with a yell when the darkness around him surged upward, a giant shaggy paw seizing him by the legs and dragging him off his feet.

"Xavier!" I reached for my wand and pointed it at the monster, but my hastily cast freeze-frame spell missed and bounced off the hillside instead. "Let go of him!"

The monster outright ignored me and continued to drag Xavier downhill by his feet. I cast a lullaby spell next, but that spell missed too. My hand was shaking too badly to aim properly, but I kept trying, my mind racing.

What was I supposed to do? Xavier was the one who had the upper hand when it came to afterworld monsters, and I didn't know if my spells would even have any effect if I managed to hit the target. *Think, Rory.*

"I said let him go!" This time, my spell connected with its target, but the flash of light made no impact upon the darkness. My heart sank like a stone. No regular spell worked on the afterworld or on the beasts that dwelled within—no doubt including my Biblio-Witch magic too.

Wand held aloft, I reached into my pocket and scraped for anything else that might be of use. No physical object would leave any impact on the monster, but maybe…

I pulled out a bag of firedust, which I kept in case of another vampire-related emergency.

Problem: I couldn't guarantee I'd be able to hit the beast without Xavier getting hurt too.

"Rory!" he gasped out. "Is that—sage?"

"No." *Wait… Sage.* Ghost repellent might work, but I didn't have any to hand. I just had the firedust, and for all I knew, fire would be just as ineffective as a regular spell.

My moment of hesitation cost me. Darkness swathed the hillside, and the afterworld opened around the beast, ready to swallow both the monster and Xavier alike.

"No!" My scream rang out as I leapt forward, into the darkness, driven by the desperate need not to let the monster take Xavier away from me.

I crashed into solid shadow, my hands grasping slippery fur that seemed more smoke than flesh. Losing my balance, I slid backwards off the beast as it rose upright, its clawed feet still grasping Xavier's legs.

"Rory," he gasped. "Run."

I can't. For one thing, we were in the afterworld, and I'd let go of his hand. If I went any further from him, I'd be lost.

More to the point, I'd already established that we were sticking together. If he went down, so did I.

A glint caught my eye on the ground—or what passed for ground in the shadows anyway—and I recognised Xavier's scythe, which he must have dropped. Noticing too, he tried to twist away from the teeth gripping his legs, but the beast continued to drag him into the shadows.

Without stopping to think, I crouched and grabbed the scythe myself. It weighed less than I'd expected, the sensation of its hilt more like grasping smoke than a solid object.

Heart in my throat, I held up the scythe towards the monster. "Hey! I told you to let him go."

My hands trembled, my whole body quaking as the beast turned towards me, acknowledging my presence for the first time.

"Rory," Xavier croaked. "Don't..."

"Let him go," I repeated, brandishing the scythe. "Come and get me instead."

The beast let go of Xavier with one clawed foot and swiped at me. I swung the scythe in retaliation as I retreated. Since it didn't weigh that much, I could lift it over my head with ease, and when the beast lunged in my direction, I brought the scythe down in a clumsy strike.

The monster let out a roar when the blade went straight through its leg—so loud that my body shook with the vibrations. Unable to help myself, I lowered the scythe and tried to cover my ears to keep from being deafened.

"Rory!" Xavier rolled away—he'd freed himself—and rose upright fluidly. Then he gave a gesture, and a familiar door-shaped outline appeared behind the beast.

With a growl, it shook off the blow and lunged at me again. This time when I swung the scythe, the beast flailed closer to the rapidly expanding door that Xavier had opened.

The monster lost its balance and toppled into the waiting darkness, tumbling out of sight.

Xavier watched for a moment until the door-like shape vanished into the surrounding shadows. Then he turned to me, his eyes wide. "Rory…"

"Oh. Sorry." I held out the scythe by the hilt. "Here you go."

"Don't apologise. You just saved my life." He took the scythe from me. "How did you know what to do?"

"Instinct. And watching you." My teeth chattered. "Where's Dwight?"

"We'll catch him." He clasped my hand in his other and pulled me out of the darkness.

We appeared on the hillside in daylight, right in front of Dwight. He turned to run, but Xavier released my hand and stepped through the afterworld again to reappear in Dwight's path. I remained in front, so that he was trapped between the pair of us.

"Your monster is gone," Xavier told him. "It's over."

16

Dwight sagged to the ground, and Xavier had him restrained in moments. Without his monstrous bodyguard, he'd lost all will to fight back, and the trip through the afterworld was the last straw. When we landed in front of the Grim Reaper's house, Dwight fell to his knees again and covered his head with his arms.

The Grim Reaper's shadowy form materialised in the doorway. "So you're the one who saw fit to summon a hell-beast. Explain yourself."

Dwight gibbered and cowered at the Grim Reaper's feet. With his boss occupied, Xavier took my hand and gave me a thorough once-over.

"I'm fine," I insisted. "You're the one who got dragged around by a monster."

"I'm a Reaper. I—"

"You're still not invincible," I interjected. "Don't act like you are."

He gave me a half smile. "You know, you were more than a match for that monster. You saved my neck back there."

"Are you going to tell…?" I gestured towards his boss.

"Oh yes." His smile faded, though. "He'll either be impressed or furious."

"What? That I picked up your scythe?"

"No, not the scythe," he said. "Any human can pick one up if not use it, but you… you followed me into the afterworld when you weren't even touching me. That's not something a regular human can do."

"I didn't even think of that," I admitted. "I was more focused on chasing that monster—and you."

I'd been following my instinct, like I'd said, and my desire not to let him out of my sight had superseded my own survival instincts.

"I can only assume it's because I've taken you into the afterworld myself so many times," he said. "Maybe we'd better not mention that part."

"Are you sure keeping secrets from him is the best idea?" Yes, the Grim Reaper was currently more focused on Dwight than the pair of us, but soon enough, he'd want an explanation from his apprentice.

"It's not really a secret," he said. "Humans don't normally spend that much time in the afterworld. Usually, their bodies can't handle it for long, but you've obviously built up a tolerance."

"And that's not allowed?"

"Definitely not," he said, "but there are grey areas. Technically, half-Reapers are similar. They have to build up the tolerance too."

"Like Maura?"

He inclined his head. "In a way. The afterworld itself responds to those who are familiar to it. That's… It's how Reapers are inducted into the afterworld to begin with. We're not born that way."

"Huh." I glanced towards the Grim Reaper. I had a hard time believing *he* hadn't been born exactly as he was, but had he started out human too? Were there any true Reapers at all?

I shrank back when the Grim Reaper met my eyes from beneath his hood. Leaving Dwight trembling on the floor, he swooped over to me and Xavier. "You're still here, Aurora?"

"Yes," I replied. "What are you going to do to Dwight? Edwin wanted to arrest him."

"No," he said. "He'll be sent to the afterworld to think on his mistakes for a while."

I winced. I didn't envy the guy for getting on the Grim Reaper's bad side, but he at least had earned the boss's ire. "And Terrance? I'm not sure how much of an accomplice he was."

"The other boy can stay in the police's custody," said the Grim Reaper dismissively. "Now, I'll kindly ask you to leave."

"She saved my life," Xavier said. "Rory has as much of a right to be here as I do."

"Explain."

He did, though he glossed over the part where I'd jumped after him into the afterworld. Instead, he made it sound like we'd still been on the hillside when he'd dropped the scythe and I'd picked it up to brandish at the beast. Even then, the Grim Reaper regarded me with a long stare that made me feel as if his invisible eyes were boring right into my soul.

"What?" I finally asked. "If you think I should have left Xavier to die, we're going to have to disagree."

"That is not what I was going to suggest," he said. "I rather expected my apprentice to have put up more of a fight against the hellbeast."

"You're unbelievable." I threw up my hands. "When you aren't criticising one of us, you're nitpicking at the other. As if you didn't send Xavier to hunt that monster alone while knowing full well that it was dangerous to him. Was this all some kind of test?"

Xavier raised a brow at his boss. "Was it?"

"Yes. You need to focus on your duties, not on… distractions."

"You let that monster rampage around town for days in the name of teaching me a lesson?" Xavier sounded as appalled as I felt. "You can hardly criticise *me* for breaking the rules."

"The beast was contained."

"Until Dwight let it out of his summoning circle," said Xavier. "What would you have done if it'd dragged me deeper into the afterworld? Would you have intervened?"

My heart contracted at the mere thought of losing him. We'd had a close call.

"I never expected things to get to that point," said the Grim Reaper. "You have more than enough training to best a mere hellbeast."

"It seems to me that all my recent training has involved you playing mind games with me," said Xavier. "I've met enough Reapers to know that isn't the norm."

"Wrong," said the Grim Reaper. "I knew it was a mistake letting you roam all over the northwest with that rogue."

"Maura isn't a rogue," he said. "There *are* rogues out there, and you should be focused on them, not on a petty grudge against a human."

"I have nothing against Aurora."

"You could have fooled me," I put in. "You know, if Xavier had—died—I'd never have forgiven you. I'd have haunted you into your own afterlife, and don't you think of telling me that's impossible. It's not supposed to be possible for a human to do what I did either."

I clamped my mouth shut, but I'd already said too much.

In response, the Grim Reaper levelled me then Xavier with a penetrating stare. "You are extremely lucky," he said. "Both of you, though not everyone would consider themselves fortunate to have a Reaper owe them a favour. Nevertheless, you did save my apprentice's life."

What—does he mean he's indebted to me? Was this some kind of vampire-style bargain? Not that I'd be making any references to his least favourite bloodsuckers when I stood on shaky enough ground already.

"Does that mean you're going to stop dragging Xavier away on ridiculous errands whenever we try to spend time together?" I asked. "I'd be happy to return to our old bargain and forget anything you might owe me if you leave us in peace. I can give that stone Xavier gave me back too."

"Keep it," he said tersely. "But don't count on Xavier always being able to come to your aid. Xavier, you, too, should not count upon Aurora being around to save you next time."

Harsh. Still, he'd let me keep the stone, which was far more than I'd expected.

"You didn't answer her," Xavier pointed out. "When she asked if you're going to let us see one another without interference. You know that none of the errands you've dragged me on have been remotely urgent. Nor have they involved Reaping anyone's soul, which is supposed to be the point of my job."

"Don't push me, apprentice." A moment passed. "Fine. I will stay out of your way."

Relief washed over me. "That's all we asked for."

With that hair-raising encounter done, it was past time I went back to the library. The others would be worried about me.

———

"Whoa," Estelle said softly when I'd finished explaining the events of the past hour or so. "You killed that monster?"

"It was already dead. I just… wanted it to let go of Xavier."

I fidgeted on the beanbag I'd sat on in the Reading Corner, surrounded by my family members. Even Cass had come downstairs to listen, though the visible tension in the way she interacted with the others indicated that she was still smarting over Aunt Adelaide's lecture on her midnight excursion on Halloween. The manticore had supposedly recovered from its cold, but it'd woken up from a nap mid-lecture and roared so loudly that it'd scared off any remaining visitors.

The upside was that the others had been too preoccupied with Cass's antics to have long to worry about what I might be doing, and none of them had guessed that Xavier and I had gone chasing after a murderer.

"Where is Dwight now?" Aunt Candace asked from where she stood with her back to a shelf, her notebook and pen bobbing up and down at her side. "In prison?"

"With the Grim Reaper, and no, you can't talk to him." I could guess what she was thinking. "I don't know how he learned to summon that monster, but if he had help, the Grim Reaper will uncover who was responsible."

"I should hope so," Aunt Adelaide replied. "It sounds like he's got the situation in hand. Is he certain that monster is all Dwight summoned?"

"Aside from Calvin's father's ghost, yes." Not Calvin himself—I didn't think. He surely hadn't wanted Calvin to show up and potentially give away the identity of the person responsible for his death. For his many faults, Calvin had been right all along.

"Are we forgetting the part where Rory went into the afterworld?" Estelle asked. "Alone? She—Rory, you could have been… killed or worse."

"I went after Xavier," I said apologetically. "I didn't think —I mean, I forgot I wasn't touching him at the time. He told me that I must have picked up a few tricks from spending so much time around the Reapers."

"Wow." Estelle sounded faint. "It's lucky you did, or you might not have been able to get out of there."

"Try not to make a habit of it," said Aunt Adelaide. "The afterworld is no place for humans."

"Believe me—the Grim Reaper made that clear already." I'd been lucky he'd spared me a longer lecture, though he'd been a tad distracted by his prisoner. "I'd like to think it'll give me a little leverage in future. You know, the next time he tries to interrupt Xavier and me when we're on the way to the pub."

"I thought those ghastly Honeywoods ruined your last date," Aunt Candace said. "Did *they* know about that Dwight's involvement in their relative's return from the dead?"

"Of course they didn't," I replied. "They were ignorant of all of it."

Luckily for us. After all, they now had no reason whatso-ever to come back and make trouble in Ivory Beach again. We were free.

"Shame," said Sylvester, who'd perched on a shelf above. He hadn't offered any comments so far but had arrived when the others did, clearly as curious to hear my account of my trip into the afterworld as everyone else was. "We haven't had to ban a whole family from the library in a while."

"What do you mean, 'shame'?" I asked. "They wrecked the place."

"Yes, but it would have been amusing to enact the conse-quences on them if they decided to test that ban," said the owl. "For me, anyway."

I gave an eye roll. "I think we've had enough excitement already."

"Agreed," Estelle said. "I think Edwin would be happy

never to set eyes upon another Honeywood again in his life. I'm glad we don't have a coven here in Ivory Beach."

"Oh, our family is far more powerful than any coven is," said Aunt Candace.

"Except when it comes to the afterworld." I looked pointedly at Sylvester. "Is that why I didn't get an answer from the Book of Questions? I mean, that monster probably isn't within the library's knowledge."

"We don't have any books on Reapers," Aunt Adelaide confirmed. "We're required by law to hand them directly over to the Grim Reaper himself, in fact, though we've very rarely had to do that."

"I figured."

The guardian might have had some inkling of the potential trouble that was occurring elsewhere in Ivory Beach, but the ghost's destructiveness had been enough of a problem on its own. Not that Sylvester would outright admit that the fourth-floor corridor had been kind enough to keep the Book of Questions safe from the ghost. When he caught me looking at him, the owl shuffled its wings. "If you wish to ask me a question—"

"Use the book," I finished. "I get it. Never mind. I can fill in the gaps myself."

Most of them. Whatever happened with Calvin's inheritance was not our problem. The killer had been caught, the monster banished, and the library was no longer playing host to a nuisance of a ghost. Everything else could wait.

Cass gave a snort. "The Grim Reaper hasn't been doing his job right if he failed to notice a monster being summoned right here in town."

"He did know," I said. "He was trying to test whether Xavier was paying attention."

Whatever mission he'd dragged Xavier on to make sure he didn't have any way to attend the party at the library hadn't been more important at all. I hoped he'd think twice about trying the same again.

"And he endangered all of us in the process," Cass said. "What an absolute—"

"Oh, I know," I said. "I think he's going to be having second thoughts about how he's treated me now that I saved his apprentice's life."

"He'd better," Estelle said with feeling. "He's been awful to you *and* Xavier. The only good thing he did was banishing that ghost."

"And that's debateable," I said. "I mean, the ghost *wanted* to be banished to escape the consequences of his own actions."

"True, but we're all better off without him."

Aunt Candace cleared her throat loudly. "Yes, and you owe me an apology for insulting my mask."

"We already did, several times," I told her. "And you never confirmed whether it *is* cursed or not."

"Oh, it's not cursed," she said as she made to walk away. "It's possessed."

"It's—*what?*"

"That's right." She smiled over her shoulder. "It's possessed by an angry spirit. Very useful when writing about possession."

"We can't keep a possessed mask in the library!" Aunt Adelaide followed her sister's path. "Candace, you must get rid of it at once."

"Here we go." Estelle sighed. "I *knew* she was up to something. Where are you going, Sylvester?"

"None of your business, you tablespoon." He took flight up to the balcony above, while Cass gave us one last amused look and vanished too.

"Was your mum really furious at her for taking out the manticore on Halloween?" I asked Estelle in an undertone.

"Oh yes," she said. "Cass is on her last chance. No more excursions, or she has to send the creature to a colony. Personally, I think it'd be happier out in the wild than in a cage, but Cass insists that it has a delicate constitution."

I grimaced. "I bet. I'm surprised she isn't holding a grudge against me for giving her away."

"I think the fault is more with Aunt Candace," said Estelle. "Not that that's anything new. A *possessed* mask…"

My phone buzzed, and my heart lifted. "Xavier."

I'm free tonight, his message said. *The boss won't bother us.*

A grin formed on my mouth. *Finally.*

Well, I might want to avoid inviting him over for dinner until we'd dealt with the issue of Aunt Candace's possessed mask, but I'd be more than happy to go to the Black Dog instead. I sent a reply and then followed the sound of raised voices to the living quarters.

"I didn't touch your mask, Candace," Aunt Adelaide was saying. "I've been within your sight for the past hour, and frankly, I've had more important things to do the rest of the time."

"Has it gone missing?" asked Estelle. "The mask?"

"Apparently so."

Nobody was inclined to help Aunt Candace search for the missing mask, but when we returned to the front desk, I found the Book of Questions lying there in plain view. Upon its surface lay what I was fairly sure was some of the fake skin from Aunt Candace's mask.

Thanks, Sylvester. Took you long enough.

As for Xavier? Even the Grim Reaper would have a hard time standing between us when I was gaining some control over the afterworld myself. Enough that I could follow Xavier anywhere, even death itself.

The next time anyone, living or dead, tried to keep us apart, they'd have to answer to both of us.

ABOUT THE AUTHOR

Elle Adams lives in the middle of England, where she spends most of her time reading an ever-growing mountain of books, planning her next adventure, or writing. Elle's books are humorous mysteries with a paranormal twist, packed with magical mayhem.

She also writes urban and contemporary fantasy novels as Emma L. Adams.

Find Elle on Facebook at https://www.facebook.com/pg/ElleAdamsAuthor/

www.ingramcontent.com/pod-product-compliance
Lightning Source LLC
Chambersburg PA
CBHW061446210726
48287CB00007B/2388